look inward

It is a grand pleasure
to know you,
albeit in cyberspace.

Peace

Jane

Dec, 99

Maryland

EPiPHANiA

EPIPHANIA

VAHÉ KAZANDJIAN

American Literary Press, Inc.
Baltimore, Maryland

Epiphania

Library of Congress
Cataloging in Publication Data
ISBN 1-56167-533-4

Published by

American Literary Press, Inc.
8019 Belair Road, Suite 10
Baltimore, Maryland 21236

Manufactured in the United States of America

Preamble

A white seagull was flying outside my window, a cold morning in December when I decided to find and arrange the short stories I had written over the past twenty years. Although I wrote these mostly as a diary, I shared them with friends, along with the black and white pictures I took and developed in my dark room. That morning, I looked at the seagull riding the rising warm air, and decided that it was time to find these short stories.

Many were still on paper, others in "ancient" word processing programs such as WP 5.0.... In my search I also found poems I had forgotten about or, plainly forgotten that I ever wrote them! But, all fit together, a testimony of times, people, and feelings. After more than a month of search, I decided to stop looking and choose what, of the diary-type stories, I wanted to share with a wider audience. The result is this booklet, for those who may identify with the experiences.

The stories are about people, themselves, and how they changed me. Many, or parts of them, were written a decade or more ago, and I tried not to edit. It is not fair to the experience itself, to edit the past. No matter the context, place, or attitude I had, the experiences I share with you have made me a more demanding man. I still have a picture in my office taken in 1971, in Greece, when I was a boy scout. I remember my needs then; I know my needs now. The main change, I fancy, is my being shorter on time. Time I had that I do not have anymore, and the shiver I felt which I remember today. I realized that these people were the keepers of the wisdom I was hoping to reach. Thus, I have become more demanding from myself and from the quality of my interactions.

In the past twenty years, I have published many books, many scientific articles, and traveled the world as a scientist. Yet, when I was putting this booklet together, I felt that tingle upon my spine, that lightheadedness I used to experience when the experience was new, when it was charming! And perhaps it is. Perhaps it matters most to share a bit of ones own past....with himself....

Still, this book would have not taken shape without the help of Laura Pimentel, my academic works' "partner in crime." She has prepared every manuscript and book I have published in the past seven years.

Her outlook to life, and friendship, have made the tedious requirements of publishing almost enjoyable. . . .!

The Hiding Place

~ "I will write about you, one day."

He laughed. Took a long draw on his favorite Rothmans cigarette, rubbed his thin moustache with his left index, coughed, and started his truck. I looked at him disappear through a dust cloud.

~ "The man who can get you anything you _ever_ want is Abu Koko. Absolutely anything! He has connections."

It was a usual day in a historical Arabian desert city. Hot, dusty, filled with expensive cars, and Indian chauffeurs. It was a city where over night, entire forests of palm trees were "planted" by Korean crews. It was a city where I had a large apartment and a great job. It was the late seventies and I had thunder in my veins.

~ "What kind of a name is that?"

~ "Well, Armenian, of sorts... See, Abu Koko is the last of these men who make love to destiny, sometimes with much passion. He is searching for himself, in this desert."

~ "Yeah, he has been doing that for some time! And mister, Abu Koko makes love to more than destiny! Abu Koko is the last of these men."

I had to meet him. New in town, it seemed as a ritualistic requisite to have tea with Abu Koko. An Armenian in the Arabian Gulf, who had connections. An Armenian who made love to destiny. And to others. This biblical neophile in search of himself in the desert. I had to meet him.

They said he will pass by the photo studio for tea. I went there to learn about the tight community of Armenians in this Arabian Gulf city. Where Pakistani workers lived in un-climatized small abodes, and always carried a green blanket on their backs. As if they were afraid of becoming homeless after the daily siesta. Or that the desert would suddenly be covered by snow. Or perhaps, it was part of the cultural accouterment. After all, I always carried extra money in my pocket. As if I would suddenly go broke after the daily siesta, in this Arabian Gulf city.

~ "Abu Coco? Yes, what a charming man! He helped my husband to the hospital, when he hurt his back. He knew the doctor. He always checked with me afterwards, if I needed anything."

The owner of the photo studio winked at me. I knew that Abu Koko was checking with her for reasons other than bread. The lady, an Australian, always developed her pictures at this studio, I was informed. She welcomed me to town.

~ "So, how is your research, big chief?" the young studio clerk asked while searching for his cigarette lighter. " I hope that we do not have any bad diseases in the city, yes? After all, we want to go back home one piece, wealthy, and ready for marriage!"

~ "We have been in this joint for too long" another man said. "Do not pay much attention to these clowns. Their heart is in the right place, but their minds are gone.
They have smelled the sweet ambrosia of freedom, and they are drunk! See, life is best, here in the desert."

It was obvious that many of the folks I met during my first week in this desert city were happy. In an unreal way. They seemed to have what they never had before, yet I was not sure what that was. Some called it freedom, others detachment. But from what? From whom?
Many of the expatriates living in these desert cities, up and down the Saudi borders, the peninsula, the island in the Gulf waters, came to escape. For many, it was the escape from the financial limitations of their jobs. For others it was the routine grind they could not waste their lives within. Yet for others, it was the escape from the conformity to rules. Here, the technological development and people's receptivity to change were so prominent that, if within the social norms of decency and appropriateness, any idea could be tested. I was there to do public health research. And, I was about to be exposed to Abu Koko, the Armenian who checked to see if the Australian lady needed anything while her husband was supine, at the hospital.

~ " A tea for Abu Koko! Double sugar, very red!"
~ "Immediately!"

Abu Koko was a thin man in his fifties, wearing plastic slippers. He wore a two-day beard, and painter's clothes. He had long fingers and spark in his eyes. Abu Koko was a tired man, at the end of a working day. He shook my hand with his wrist—"....hands smell like turpentine" he said.

~ "So, chief, how do you like our town? I bet you have not seen the best of it yet!"
~ "Abu Koko, the Australian lady says hello."

4

~ "Yes! Yeees! Did you know that the doctor, a good friend of mine, kept him a few days extra at the hospital? Just to make sure that his back was strong again!"

All laughed. I was getting closer to understanding what the escape was all about.

~ "You came from Beirut? Pity what is happening to that city. Here, we have Armenians from Tehran, Damascus, Aleppo, and Jordan. We even once had a big chief from America. An expert of sort. He was here for a week. We cooked kebabs for him, had good whiskey, and fine company. But, I think that the meat was not cooked enough for him. He spent most of his days here throwing up! I think that people in America are not resistant to microbes. What do you think?"

Abu Koko was charming as a rogue man, as a kind man. He was known to lend a hand with no expectations. Of course, unless they had expectations! "I always keep in touch, afterwards," he said "the city center is five blocs, you know. We eventually meet again."

But Abu Koko was also an aching man. Abu Koko once cried in his room. He had invited me and another Armenian doctor for kebab. And sprits, both distilled and wounded. Those of Armenian expatriates from their former immigration lands of Lebanon, Syria, Iran, Jordan. He promised the best lamb cuts, the freshest liver, and great company. It was seven of us, all male, invited to his apartment.

Abu Koko's apartment consisted of a bed, a small table, and a couple of pictures of Koko, his son. Although that night we did not ask him about his son, he often looked at the picture through a wet eye, after a few drinks. It was never clear if his eyes watered from the smoke drifting into his room from the charcoal grill on the small balcony. Or his chain smoking of Rothmans cigarettes. Or just the memory of that part of him, left behind.

On the small table, Abu Koko had a radio-TV-video and cassette player monster boom-box. The 5 inch B&W TV was his favorite gadget. He had tapes of singing girls from Singapore; belly dancers from Egypt; and soap operas from India. But his favorite tapes were from Beirut, of Armenian gatherings and celebrations. And that night, while rotating the dozens of shish-kebabs on his grill perched on the concrete railing of his balcony, Abu Koko showed us the tape of Koko.

5

The picture was bad. But we could see Koko, a twenty-some years old young man, dancing Armenian folkloric dances. His back was straight, his chest proud, and his hand waved a white handkerchief. The sign of the dance leader. Abu Koko kept flipping the shish kebabs, and poured whiskey to all in the room. Abu Koko had connections. Abu Koko could get anything he wanted, from whiskey to good company.

Except that he could not get his Koko back. The last few minutes of the tape were scenes from the Armenian cemetery of Beirut. On a rainy day.

~ "The box was empty, chief," Abu Koko said "the shell fell right next to him. Nothing of Koko was left. Except this tape. All I have to show, after 25 years."

We drank to Koko, the young man who danced Armenian folkloric dances, with a straight back. And we drank to Abu Koko, an Armenian who crouched under the weight of pain. And I understood why Abu Koko was in the desert. I understood what freedom he was talking about. I understood why his friend, the Sudanese doctor, kept the back patient two days longer than usual. Abu Koko was among the last of men who made love to destiny, and never peace with the past. Abu Koko could get a taste of Emir's dinner (the cook was his friend..), but will not see Koko dance the proud dance again, hitting the floor hard with his red booths, and waving the white handkerchief in pride. No, Abu Koko was a thin, tired man in his fifties, who had nothing else to lose.

I stayed in that city for about two years. Abu Koko became both a friend and an aging man. But he kept his reputation of "having rooster in his genes" intact. For some unknown reason, by some unknown means, Abu Koko befriended, "more than once", many of the new comer women in the city. And for that, and that gift alone, we often stood up and saluted him, when he entered the room. He liked that. So did we.

And then, my "freedom" had to end. I had a path to find, while Abu Koko and his disciples had found theirs. I wanted to deal with my own sour memories of the war, of lost friends, of lost innocence, differently. We had two weeks of seemingly interminable celebration.

~ "This is it, chief, he said. I will not see you again."

~ "Nonsense, I will be back."

6

~ "No. Once you leave, you leave. People do not come back to the desert."

And, the day I was leaving for the airport, Abu Koko drove in his pick up truck to my place. He was a thin, tired man in his fifties wearing painter's pants and hat.

~ "We had good times, eh chief?"

~ "Yes, Abu Koko, we did. And I will write about you one day" I said.

He smiled.

~ "Just don't tell them everything, eh chief?"

~ "Promised, Abu Koko."

And he left. While he was walking toward his truck, I realized that Abu Koko had gotten old. And, I think that he may had dried a tear with the back of his hand, while covering his mouth from the cough.

—*April 28, 1997*

Why the Bloody Brain, Love?
(A Christmas Story)

~ "I do not trust seat belts. They are often so dirty that I get a dark line on my shirt. Just drive well. Too many roundabouts, you know. Grand. Nice of you to pick me up. Armenian, you said, love? Never met an Armenian before."

I was chaperoning her to a party given by the Australian public health team. My sport car was immaculately clean, and she was an Irish nurse with an attitude. I was hoping that the Australian nurses would be much more fun. I remember it being a bright night, in the Arabian desert. It was 1981 and I was young.

Philomena was a tall, attractive, jovial Irish woman with enough love to intoxicate most of Dublin 16, her residence area, back home. For now, she was in the Arabian Gulf, discovering a microcosm of human realities like she never thought she would. In an unpredictable and unplanned for way, she was part of an untraditional world, created almost spontaneously and racing to catch up with its times. A world where money was able to buy the potential for quick development--the prerequisite for social puberty. Since the mid-70's, many countries of the Arabian Gulf had invested in the development of technology and medical care. Both seen as good investments into a future upon which most people were sitting-- the fields of oil, the fluid and volatile fields of dream. Fluid like the ordinary joys one experiences when in search of joy itself, in desert towns where time is often tardy. And volatile as the international interest was in transforming the traditional times into a present already living its promising future. Given the pace at which the fields of dreams were parading on the shores of the Arabian Sea and Persian Gulf, these countries seemed unreal, just as the dreams themselves. Otherwise, a good mirage shared by many. Simultaneously.

We were these dreamers. We were the expatriates invited to help the country develop the best systems money could buy. Systems for care and caring; systems for medical research. Many of us went there for the opportunity to partake in a true metamorphosis--of the people and their environment. Some were there to experience a metamorphosis they could not achieve back home: that of their own self. I met Philomena during these days, in my sport car, on our way to the Australian team party, on a bright night in the Arabian Gulf. I was asked to give her a lift, to the party.

~ " Let's draw the curtains down, love" Phil said, "let's pretend it is snowing!" Phil had the best Christmas parties, in a Moslem country, where alcohol is for cleaning wounds, not for soothing bleeding souls. But there was always plenty of spirits chez Phil, many entrapped in bottles, in cans, even in orange juice bottles... Phil was a senior government consultant, and an infidel. So was I. We, and a number of other expatriates, were given an "alcohol ration" by the government, monthly. Any kind you wished, just do not share or sell to Moslems. If you do, you will be escorted to the first plane, to home. Where there is plenty of alcohol but often no dreams. Your choice.

~ "Let's dance, kiss the year goodbye." We did so, a handful of expatiate health professionals for two years, during Christmas and the rest of the year. Phil was our leader, a woman born for friendship, love of life, ever pleasant, ready to discover, ready to dance. And she did so for the following 15 years I knew her. When I kissed her goodbye, on an ordinary day in a desert town, she said: "America is new but you have an old soul. Will you be comfortable there?" I promised to let her know. I did so when we met again in Dublin, years later. I did so in my letters, over the phone, in my writings. I told her that people had old souls in America. From her home in Dublin, she often answered "You will be a romantic, forever." And signed her letters with a typically Irish sarcasm: "Eventually Yours, Phil."

It was one of these letters that I opened a September day, in 1995. "Dearest friend, I have brain cancer. The galloping type. But no worries, I am ready." She never said that she would beat the disease; she knew what was happening in her skull. She was an Irish nurse with an attitude. An attitude toward life and destiny. An attitude for fighting good battles. This was not one of them.

~ "Why not breast or uterus?" she once said over the phone, "why the bloody brain?" But she quickly changed topic, asked about the kids, if America was right for me, if I was still falling in love. Phil was herself, no matter what happened to her, as long as a friend was around. " I was gardening, and suddenly my arm went numb. I thought it was from the bad Cork gin" she joked. "But I knew. Too many headaches lately. Pity, just before Christmas! You know how

9

much I love that time of the year. Oh, Vahé, you should be here: the snow is just gorgeous. May be we can dance again. For the Irish; for the Armenians. For all those who saw snow in the desert. Remember?"

I called her sister. "Nuala, I would like to come and see Phil. It has been eight years. Just for a couple of days. What do you say?"

~ "No, love, just write to her. She is in pain, and taking it beautifully. But she would not want you to see her. You do not want to see her."

So, I wrote to her, and called her. And when she could not talk anymore, I just wrote to her. Nuala read my letters to her. Phil dictated a few words back to me. That way, I was with her, the Phil before cobalt, radium radiation, before she was bold, before her speech was gone, before her arms were limb, before she could not have gin on the rocks, gin on gin. Before she could not smile the most gorgeous smile I have ever seen on a woman, or a man. Before she died, a few days before Christmas of 1995.

....Today, December 13, 1996, I am thinking about Phil. It is very early in the morning, my daughter is having tubes inserted in her ears (this time by the ENT guy, not her brother...); my son is ill with the flu and throwing up every 15 minutes on the kitchen linoleum floor; it is pouring rain outside and my dog is asking to go out. I almost feel like having a gin and tonic. A tall one. For Phil.

Instead, I brewed coffee, rather strong coffee to make me sick to the stomach. And, listened to the rain. On the wood, on the asphalt, on the car top. On my soul. It is raining in me, this mourning of Phil. I looked at the Christmas tree Janet and the kids decorated a week ago. Time to share, time to dance, time to love. Phil will not do so, this year. Nor the next. Never. Instead, there will be an Armenian boy, somewhere in America, who in his old soul, will remember Phil, the Irish nurse with an attitude. I will remember her as the angel atop the imaginary Christmas tree we had in her small apartment, in the Arabian desert. And I will always wonder, how did she manage to say "I love you, love" to her doctor, her nurse, her sister and the hospice staff when her speech was gone, and the arms were limp.

I think she just smiled, and they knew.

—*February 15, 1997*

10

Ronald

~ "I was chased by a bloody camel" he said "perhaps it was the red shirt I was wearing."

Ronald was a Scott, like no Scott I ever met. He seemed the embodiment of all character traits known by others to be Scottish.

It was the Persian Gulf in its glory days —summer of 1982. Doha, the capital of Qatar, where I was located, was a booming city where the Arabian dhows and IBM super computers coexisted amid a social structure ridden by time-tested traditions.

Ronald was a communications expert, some sort of an engineer responsible for weaving a communications web across the desert and into the major cities of Qatar. He and his crew, mostly Pakistani workers, were in Dukhaan when a camel chased Ronald, rather viciously. While running away, he fell and seemed to have hurt his back. He had scorched palms and forehead from the abrasive encounter with the desert sand. But it was his pride that needed healing.

I was at the Rumaillah Hospital discussing issues of primary care with an Egyptian physician when they brought Ronald.

She was a very pale, slightly overweight, very attractive woman. I noticed her first in the lobby of the Sheraton hotel, wearing the colors of the car rental agency. It was a day like all other days in the easy flow of time in the desert. She was pale and overweight, with a large smile and conversant eyes. She smiled every morning when I came down to the lobby, in a memorable way. She always fixed her British colors scarf with the right hand and leaned her head to the left. That was unusual, during those usual days.

~ "Are you a doctor?" She once asked "You look like you could be."

I was young, very young, and my blood boiled easily. We chatted every day, about things one would only chat about when encountering a pale, overweight woman in a desert town. We often talked about my hobby for cooking, spear fishing, and fast cars. I was very proud of my German car, and she knew the reliable mechanics in town.

That morning she came to the hospital and looked worried.

11

~ "Is Ronny here?" She said "I am so glad to find you here.".

~ "He was attacked by a camel" I said "but the poor beast will survive."

~ "He is well then? Good, I was worried."

I was invited to their house that night. She was even more attractive in her casual clothing. It was a funny situation, since Ronald decided that he would lay on the floor, on his belly, while we sat down next to him and ate from the plate on our lap. He asked me if it was better for his back to lay down as such, and I said yes. She was the perfect hostess, although slightly old fashioned in her behavior. She was not the professional woman I met every morning; she was Ronny's wife and the cook for that night. She let Ronald behave like the man of the house, even after being chased by a bloody camel. It was better that way, she said, "relationships with camels do not last long." After 13 years, I still find that reaction charming.

He smoked good cigars, or at least he said they were. A few times that evening, I was inclined to say "It is even better if you lay on your belly and go to sleep."

But I did not.

I talked to her every morning, for more than three months. Then, I was transferred to a different location and passed by the hotel rather infrequently. Till the night of January 23, 1983.

It was a cold night, like the cold is in the desert. Perhaps for the first time, I had turned the heat on in my car. I finished my daily squash game, sweat in the sauna, jumped into the pool, and took a long shower. I was feeling young, filled with vigor, and ready for something new.

I met with the guys, as we did most evenings. We talked about the day for a few minutes and then about women for a long time. It was custom; it was how things were. On a lucky evening, or noon siesta time, some of us would have other plans. And that, was the topic of the next gathering, and sometimes even the one after. Perhaps it was the desert reaching into the sandy beaches of the Persian Gulf; perhaps it was the smell of goat skin rugs in the Pakistani stores. I think it was the youth in us. Whatever it was, we liked it.

On January 23, 1983, I went home alone, after meeting with the guys. I had a sore wrist from hitting the wall hard on the squash court. I also had a 16 year old bottle of single malt Scottish whiskey, courtesy of a local friend. I had planned to listen to classical music, smell the coolness of the desert in January, and taste the single malt. There was a three quarters of a moon hanging somewhere as if lost with no reference point. Indeed, the dunes may change, when the winds are right.

I was half asleep, hugging my pillow and dreaming of spear fishing, when knocks on my door erupted, with no apparent cadence. My first reaction was to ignore them: once before, almost a year ago, one of my neighbors fell onto my door creating an imposing blasting sound. He was still on the floor when I opened the door: he apologized and, albeit with some difficulty in concentration, he opened his door and disappeared. I never asked what was wrong with him: those days, we never did.

But I did not ignore the knocks. Without turning the living room lights on, I opened the door. She was there, for the first time at my door, pale, very pale. Actually she was shaking, on this very cold January night. I looked at her for a long time. She was out of context, she <u>was</u> her own context. Everything else seemed nomadic, passing, temporary and, comparable to my dream about spear fishing. There was always a waking up from them. Not from her. That was 13 years ago, and I still see her face in the twilight of my third level apartment hallway, on a cold January night, in the Persian gulf desert.

~ "They followed me" she said.

I ushered her into my apartment. I had never seen her off guard; she looked older, and somewhat embarrassed.

~ "Who are they? And what are you doing out at this hour? Where is Ronald?"

I remember feeling uneasy about the whole thing, myself. I hardly had anything on, I was half asleep, she was in my living room, and her husband was a strong Scott. (He had a bad back, but I did not think about it then.) What was she doing in the city at this hour? This was the Persian Gulf, where women did not drive cars, or go out without a man.

~ "Ronald is in Saudiyyah" she said "he will be back tomorrow. I was driving back from a female friend's house. At the Oasis Hotel roundabout, this car started following me. They flashed their lights, and drove very near my car."

~ "Who are they?"

~ "How would I know? I was trying to get out of their way, not to investigate their motive."

~ "Where are they now?"

~"In the street, parked behind my car."

Behind her car! So they know she is here. Perhaps they know she is married, and that I am not her husband. Perhaps they will just call the police, and have us arrested for adultery. My spear fishing dream scenes had changed into one where I was escorted, along with my Scottish friends into the airport to leave a country I loved but did not abide by the simplest of the rules: no adultery.

But wait. That rule was for inter-religious relationship. It did not apply to us, we were both Christians, we were both infidels! I remember feeling more comfortable with her presence at this point.

I was about to ask her to sit down when two man, wearing the local attire, showed at my door. In the confusion, the door was left open. They had short sticks in their hands, a sight I recall with discontent.

One of them addressed me in English, asking if this woman was my wife. I refused to answer and asked them to leave. I was feeling protective, somewhat proud of having her in my custody. Sort of a primordial feeling, I guess. It was the desert, the moon, the poorly lit hallway where two man, in white robes, were asking me in a broken English about a very pale woman in my living room

I told them that it was none of their business. I responded in English, because any discussion in Arabic would have serious consequences: they could have called the police. It would have taken many hours to clarify that I was an infidel. Meanwhile, my reputation as a senior advisor to the Minister of....

Not good. I continued to answer in English and raised my voice in hope to get my neighbors out of their happy midnight slumber. But in those day, no one wanted to get involved.

I remember my knees shaking, and I remember her moving towards me, behind me, and finding refuge from the moment. It took me a few minutes to realize that the two young man were policeman. They had followed her because she was a single woman driving. They were worried that she will get into trouble! What a relief! I thanked them for their caring and wished them goodnight

~ "She is home now" I said "She will be fine."

At this, one of the two man, already a step down on the stairs, looked back and said, in Arabic(!)

~ "Who do you think we are, doctor? We know you. Enjoy the night!" And winked.

I was embarrassed, but also amused. Early that evening I was ready for something new, and the gods of the wind, sand, sea, and cool desert nights had heard my wish. I was a happy Armenian.

It was the early hours of the morning already, and I made tea, served her toast. I even had some caviar, but she refused.

~ "Only chicken eggs for me."

I did not have any of these cheap avian products in my refrigerator.

I cannot recall all that we said, but I think it was mostly an embarrassing moment for her. She thanked me for my help, and was ready to leave.

~ "Again? Don't you know the rules? Why not stay here tonight?"

I was sincere about my invitation, and had no other expectations. At that moment, she was not a woman: she was an unusual creature, in an unusual place.

And she did. First, she looked long into my eyes, and then smiled.

~ "You are a kind man" she said.

I was primarily enchanted.

She slept in the guest room. I went back to my room, and laid flat on my belly. The moon was filtered through the curtains above my bed and I could feel the chill in the house. The desert cold was really of a different kind. I remember thinking about the woman next room, about her being there, about her husband being in Saudiyyah. And then, I should have gone back to sleep.

The uninviting sound of the alarm clock woke me up. I opened my eyes and for a moment, could not dissociate reality from my dream. It was a dream, I knew, that Ronald's wife was in my apartment last night. It was a dream that two white robed man spoke in English to me. It was a dream that..

No it was not. I jumped out of bed, almost ran to the guest room. I slightly pushed the door, and looked through. The bed was made and the room was empty. But I could smell a woman. Someone had been there, someone <u>was</u> there, that is for sure.

I walked to the kitchen, and found a pot of coffee made, with toast and caviar on the side. And there was a note:

15

~ "Please accept Ronny's and my invitation for dinner, any night, at your convenience."

I did not have dinner with her nor Ron. I avoided going to the Sheraton Hotel for many months. And then, I heard that they had left the country. Deported, said the newspaper. I was intrigued. I called a friend of mine at the ministry of health, visa divisions. "What happened, Hitmi?"

~ "Well, the son-of-a-bitch was not married: his "wife" was his sister! They falsified the forms. We checked their place: only one bed! Do you think they slept together?"

That I don't know. But I was glad that she left that note in my kitchen, and nothing else.

—May 12, 1996

Zaven

~ "I discovered we have something in common. We both once were bodybuilders."
It was late in the day when I read her e-mail. Kept looking at the screen and thinking about a prompt reply. She was young, sharp, pleasant, and attractive. My mind flew to the old country where I once was her age. And....
~ "When you do push-ups, think about pushing down hard, as if you're digging in the dirt. Then you can, for a few seconds, pull away and be hands free. Then you can even clap. Twenty five push ups will be just right! You first learn to throw your body up, before throwing the ball in the air."
His name was Zaven. A solid-built athlete. His body was not sculptured. He had disproportionately large biceps and pectorals for any woman to envy. His hips were minuscule compared to his shoulders. He also walked with an exaggerated pointing of the toes. In some ways, Zaven was a little Popeye, and a very gauche tap dancer.
But he was best known for his character, Zaven the shot putter. He was a model for us, high school seniors, brown-eyed boys and girls. Zaven did not smoke, excessively drink, or tell sexually explicit stories. He was too self confident for such show-off. Zaven was a shoe maker by day, and an iron-pumping maniac by night. He also dedicated his free time to training young athletes, being their big brother.
Zaven had a very hairy chest. "It keeps my heart warm" he explained. We knew his wonderfully large heart needed a large chest. A hairy one. And many friends. Zaven was a champion, and I wanted to be one.
It was around 1972. I already was a medal wearing, trophy collecting collegial table tennis player and intra-mural champion. I also was at the peak of my testosterone production. It was the time when all my muscles engorged with blood very frequently. And got bigger easily. It was that time in every boy's life, when the center of the world has the shape of a gonad. When veins pop out of your forearms; when you use aftershave before you shave. It was the

perfect time for bodybuilding. And I decided to bulk up, become a power athlete.

In less than two years, I proudly displayed small trophies for shot putt, javelot, and hammer throwing accomplishments. I became large, and also powerful. In fact, at the high school or boy scout's annual "kermesses" (faire), I used to be challenged, as if a strange creature, in arm wrestling by coupon holders...

~ "Vahé, Dr.. Soandso. You're available?"

~ "Vahé?"

~ "Yes, sure" I replied almost shouting into the phone's inter-com box. "Yes, I'm here."

I was suddenly 25 years older, somewhere in Lutherville, Maryland. The call was transferred and I discussed a clinical research protocol.

Then hang up. Tilting my chair back, looked at the computer screen. Her message was still there "We have something in common...."

....It was Spring of 1974. The stadium was full. Perhaps five thousand people. Perhaps three thousand. It was a huge crowd, in the old country, next to the Mediterranean sea. The bluest of them all. Yes, that was a memorable crowd, a memorable day. The sky was high, so were our hopes for victory. I was part of the athletic team, representing a prominent Armenian athletic club.

I was the shot putter. I had been doing well, those days, with the 7.5 kilogram iron ball. That morning, my arm felt very well. On and off, I pumped myself up, with a dumbbell, with the iron ball. I was ready.

The youngest athlete in shot putt competition, I had formidable opponents. At least three of them were capable of throwing beyond 11 meters. One had once even reached the 14 meter mark. An impossible target for me. But I was young, a bodybuilder, did not smoke, did not drink. I was popular at parties, and with girls. Anything was possible, that warm day in the old country.

I finished fourth. I did well, but three others did better. It was a good competition, but I lost. "There are no happy losers" Zaven often told us, "just ones who think happy thoughts. About the next competition. The next projectile leaving the palm of their hand, scratching their neck, and chin. There are no happy losers."

18

I remember sitting down on the sand, feeling the sun on my neck, my tired arm, on my face. The games were over, and I would not climb on the podium. Not for first, not for second, not for third place. I would be a spectator, one who celebrates others' victories.

~ "Vahé, you're throwing the disc."

What disc? I was not the discobole! But, the chap who knew how to throw that wood and iron pancake was throwing up on the side of the field. He was sick like a 9 year old goat.

~ "But I cannot throw a disc!" I protested.

~ "You have thrown everything else away, so far. We need to remain in the competition."

I was again on the field, among the competitors. It felt good. I was young, and my blood boiled easily. The disc throwing was the last competition of the day.

(These days I preferred to compete in a "throwing" competition later in the afternoon. Somehow, it was that geste of reaching for the stars that crowned a day with glory. Not the medal around the sweaty neck. I often imagined a star and tried to hit it. With the iron ball. With the javelot. Curiously, I have never stopped aiming at these imaginary stars... Never reached one yet..)

I looked around. There were a few reporters, with their summer hats and large cameras. Sort of Arabic Paparazzi's. Other athletes were also on the field; the runners were bare feet, relaxing after the run; and the jumpers were protesting a seemingly wrongful arbitration. I think that in those days, athletic competitions were limited to throwers, runners, and jumpers!

I remember holding the disc in my palm, slightly bending my wrist inward, and placing the metal rim on the inside of my forearm. I had no mastery of the rotation technique: I knew the basics, the very basics. I knew that the best trajectory follows a departure at a 45 degree angle. I knew that the rotating had to be harmonious, to add momentum to the throw. I knew that the disc should become an appendage of your body, not a foreign object. I knew how to throw an iron ball. But a disc....

I almost killed one reporter! I vaguely member launching the disc. It departed too low, too early. Too gauche. It flew like a frisbee, at a six foot height, straight toward the reporters, on the sidelines of the field! Not even toward the fan-shaped area of throw, in front of me.... Toward that one who had a camera in his face, pointed at me. He probably thought I had a chance of doing something worth reporting, worth taking a picture of the throw. Perhaps a new regional record would be established. Instead, I almost beheaded him. With a spinning disc, with a rusty iron band around it. He was lucky that his colleague had quick reflexes. To throw him down. On his camera! Shouting a highly colorful cuss, for my ability to throw. For the mother of my coach; for the souls of two of my immediate ancestors! I still remember that colorful language, twenty five years later....

....That was my last competition as an amateur athlete. Life had other challenges for me, for my generation. Civil war, death of friends, career decisions, and dark hair girls. The competition was for survival, in a world of Armenians in an Arab world. In a world of Armenians in a non-Armenian world.

~ "Vahé, you're late for picking up the kids!"

It was my assistant, on the voice box. I was back to the world of research and corporate structures. I was back to Maryland, just south of the Mason-Dixon line....

Yes, the twins! I have a son and a daughter. And I need to pick them up from school...

~ "Goodness, Laura, I have to run!!"

~ "See me first."

On my way out, I stopped by her desk.

~ "You ok?"

~ "Sure. A young woman was asking about my sculptured body!" I relied.

~ "Yeah, sure" Laura said. "Go. You do not want to be the last dad to pick the kids. And, remember, tomorrow you have the obstetrics panel."

....A few minutes later, stuck in rubber-necking traffic on the Baltimore Beltway, I was wondering about Zaven's fate. And, unconsciously, put my left hand upon my right biceps. I smiled, and started thinking about an answer, an honest one, through the e-mail, to my ex-bodybuilder colleague....

—*October 23, 1996*
American Airlines Flight #1551
Baltimore to Dallas-Fort Worth

Daddy's Girl

~ "Could you get me a pillow?" she said. "I will need one for the trip."

~ "Sure, and a blanket too?"

~ "Just a pillow, thank you."

Row 5, Aisle seat. A collection of tired faces around me. "Not a full flight" I was told, "take any seat you want." The aisle seat was mine, and I was happy with it.

I gave her a pillow, and noticed the color of her hair. It was a peculiar blond, with a lot of shades. Perhaps it was the reading light spotted on it. Or perhaps my eyes were tired from the day. I sat down, buckled my seat belt, and searched for my glasses in my coat pocket. She looked like a model. Perhaps not from "Victoria's Secrets" but definitely from Hechts.

I tried to ignore my pleasure from having a model-look-alike sitting next to me. It was late in the evening and I was coming back to Baltimore.

~ "Flight attendants prepare the cabin for departure."

It has been a rewarding day. A presentation to a health care system in St. Louis, and no flight delays. Perhaps I could be home at a reasonable hour and have some time to chat with my wife.

~ "Smooth take off" she said.

~ "Yes" I replied "sometimes it can be jerky."

~ "I feel the rough rides more now that I am pregnant" she said.

~ "Congratulations! First baby?"

~ "Third pregnancy" she rushed to answer, "the other two were not successful."

~ "Sorry to hear that. How is this one going?"

I realized that my friendliness was welcomed. She was eager to talk. The plane reached the required altitude and the cabin lights dimmed. She had the reading light still shining on her peculiar blond hair. She asked the passenger in Row 6 if he would mind having her seat back. "I feel more comfortable that way" she told him. The gentleman decided to change seats since the flight was half full. "You be comfortable now" he said while leaving his seat.

On my Dictaphone, I recorded remarks about my meeting, and a few other personal issues. "Send report about infection rates;

article on Cesarean section; follow up with phone call to corporate office. Tomorrow, give dog's heart worm pill."

She was leafing through the flight magazine. I noticed that she had no interest in reading any of the articles. It is almost an instinctual behavior of every tired passenger to pick up the magazine, go through the pages with hazy eyes, and place it back into the front seat's back pocket. More, it is almost a ritual. I believe that the most tired passengers also read the folded brochure where the emergency exits, and "No Smoking" regulations are described. And they do so on every flight. I think it makes them feel more prepared in case there is a need to evacuate the plane.

I closed my eyes and just wanted to be there. But I also wanted to be courteous to my flight companion.

~ "Returning home?" I asked.

~ "No. Visiting for a short time. I have a date with the father of my child."

There was a smile in her voice. A pretty smile, I thought.

~ "Husband or friend?"

~ "Not husband. A real good friend. I am not sure if I want him for husband. That's why I am going to Baltimore."

She was perhaps 26 years old. In men's size, I estimated her shoulders to fit a 42R jacket. I couldn't guess her height but perhaps 5'10" would be right.

~ "You ordered vegetarian meal?" asked the flight attendant.

~ "Yes" she replied. "I cannot stand the taste of regular airline meals. I am pregnant."

~ "Congratulations!" Sally replied. (I always read the flight attendants' name tag.)

~ "And you sir, also a vegetarian meal?"

~ "Isn't that a coincidence," my travel companion exclaimed. "You do not eat red meat?"

~ "I do, but mostly lamb. I am Armenian." I said, as if only Armenians ate lamb. (It was sort of a joke, but she didn't pick up on it.)

~ "You know how much fat there is in red meat?"

(Yes, but I was not interested about a lecture on red meat. Sometimes I felt that there was too much emphasis on red meat consumption, especially from those who eat french fries and premium ice cream.)

~ ".... Also, they say pork is the other white meat! Gimme a break! They say 20 percent less fat. Less than what? One hundred percent?"

~ "All things in moderation are ok" I replied. "We are omnivorous , you know." (I think that "omnivorous" meant as much to her as "Armenian" had a few moments ago.)

~ "Well, even before my pregnancy, I couldn't afford much body fat. I did compete, you know."

~ "Yeah? What kind of competition?"

~ "I am a model and a body builder. Often the two go well together. Free weights do a lot of good to your body, you know."

~ "Yes, I do. About competition, what was your fat to muscle ratio?"

~ "You know about body building. At my best it was 11 percent body fat," she indirectly answered to my question.

~ "Impressive. When I was young, my best was 13 percent. I did not compete though. Just did a lot of athletics."

~ "And now, what do you do? Are you a doctor?"

~ "Health care researcher" I said. "But I know a thing or two about medicine."

The cabin was very dim. I could hear two distinct snores from the back seats. My companion was shining under the reading spot light, and I couldn't resist asking.

~ "I am curious, is this the natural color of your hair?"

~ "Yes. My entire family has great hair. I am part Swede and part German. A good combination I guess."

~ "And where are you from?"

~ "Bismarck, North Dakota. But I have been all over the place."

I realized that within less than half an hour she had told me things I had no desire to know. But, the flight was a long one, and I was tired of the day. "It was like watching mindless T.V." I thought "just look at her." (I neglected the fact that I do not -usually- talk back to a TV set!)

~ "You know, I got pregnant only after two months of my last miscarriage?"

Should I get involved in this conversation? Oh, why not? She wants to talk, I'd listen. Besides, I was beginning to enjoy the obvious spontaneity of this young woman. Clearly, she was not shy, nor seemed to suffer from complexes so dear to some of my psychologist friends.

~ "That seems quite soon," I tried evasively.

~ "Tell me about it! I was not using anything, you know. They told me nothing could happen for a while after the miscarriage."

~ "Did you get a D&C?" I asked.

~ "No. It just happened. It was not pretty, but really, not a big deal. What I couldn't understand is this pregnancy so shortly after."

~ "Well obviously...."

The flight attendant saved me from the hypothesis I was about to propose.

~ "Vegetarian for Mr. K-A-Z..."

~ "If you cannot read it, it is me," I replied to her.

The meal provided a moment of respite. But really, just a moment.

~ "This bean dish really smells!" I heard. "I cannot take certain smells nor spicy food. I used to, but now.."

~ "What would you like to drink?" asked Sally.

~ "Tomato juice" I said, "no ice."

~ "Perrier for me. With ice."

(I never understood the logic of ordering "designer water" and mixing it with solidified airline water.)

~ "I couldn't drink tomato juice from a can" she continued, "It gives me acidity. I like fresh fruit juices, though. When freshly squeezed, they are not as acidic."

~ "I don't mind" I said, "I am Armenian."

More than an hour to go and the story of her life was not over yet. She was a nice change from ordinary travel companions who often do not notice you, or talk about the color of the sky, or make jokes they only find funny (perhaps like the "I am Armenian" statement?) Also, I had read the same flight magazine more than three times this month. There were no more adds I wanted to cut out, either.

~ "So, what do people do in Bismarck?" I asked.

~ "My family lives on a farm there. It is beautiful country you know."

~ "Actually I do" I replied. "I have been to Deadwood, South Dakota, and the Black Hills. Great outdoors!"

~ "Oh, yeah. Funny little town, Deadwood!"

~ "And what do people do in Bismarck?" I revisited.

24

~ "Oh, not much. Personally, I love to shoot pool" she replied, happy realizing that I started this conversation, for a change.

~ "That can be fun. I have tried it a few times myself."

~ "Are you any good at it? I am really a good pool player. I play with the guys and they hate it when I win."

How much could I talk about pool shooting? It was not even an activity that I found attractive. But, it was better than hearing about her pregnancy history, so I continued to be pleasant.

~ "Do you have a pool shooting partner?"

~ "No. I just go to the bar in the evening, and challenge the guys. Ah, you should know that one reason they go crazy is that I like to shoot pool wearing a short skirt and high heels."

(Why should I know about that?)

~ "Is that the common apparel in North Dakota?"

~ "No. I feel comfortable wearin 'em. But now, with this pregnancy.."

(Yes, what a change in life style!)

~ ".... Now I frequently need to keep my feet higher than my heart. My doctor said that I should sleep with my legs up. I tried a couple of pillows under 'em, and that really feels good."

~ "I am glad" I said. "You should take all possible initiatives for comfort."

The lady sitting in the front seat was obviously distracted by our conversation. For the first time in more than an hour, turned her head back and looked at us. I could read "Do I need to hear all this?" in her eyes.

But my travel companion was unaffected. She had paid for the ride and she would talk about her pregnancy if she wanted to.

~ "I see varicose veins on my legs already" she picked up the conversation. "My sister had the same problem. Only, she never lost the weight she put on. I will. Also, I am eating a lot of rabbit food. They say a pregnant woman can get irregular."

(I was really happy that she was eating lots of roughage and was not irregular yet.)

~ "Good" I said. "You probably know the right exercises for returning to your previous shape and functions."

~ "Yes, that is no problem. I am worried, though. If I need a c-section, then the scar will not allow me to compete."

~ "You do not have to have a c-section" I said. "Many a times it is a discretionary decision."

~ "You know quite a bit about these things, don't you?"

~ "I am a researcher."

~ "Of course. So, tell me what else do you know?"

~ "Well, are you visiting your doctor or nurse as scheduled?

~ "No. I called the clinic in Bismarck. They told me to come and see them after my tenth week. I am not sure that is ok. Do you?"

~ "You have not seen any health professional since the beginning of your pregnancy?"

~ "No. I have two more weeks to go. But I am going to be in Baltimore during that time and do not have a doctor there."

Was it youth or ignorance? I felt like discussing some of the issues with her but refrained from it. After all, I knew little about the woman sitting next to me.

~ "What about vitamins? Folic acid?"

~ "I take a multivitamin tablet and mineral supplement everyday. But I started it without anyone telling me what to do."

~ "It seems to me that finding about a different doctor may be a good thing to do."

~ "Well, I am doing well. And besides, I don't like doctors."

~ "That is no excuse" I said. "You do not have to like everyone you meet. Some things need to be done, that's all."

~ "Perhaps. I will check with my friend when I see him in Baltimore."

Healthcare is something I know about and I was glad that she embarked on that topic. But, not for long.

~ "He is really chicken" she said looking away, through the window. "He says that he wants to marry me, but then does not want to pay for my health insurance nor the pregnancy expenses. I am even not sure if I want him to. It is my baby, you know. I am the one eating crackers in bed at two in the morning and feel like puking on every flight!"

(What a wonderful criterion.)

~ "What does your friend do?"

~ "He is a pilot. We met seven months ago in Buenos Aires. He is away a lot, so am I. But, we have been faithful to each other in the past months. I have. He tells me he is not seeing anyone else either."

I smiled. I knew where my limits of inquiry or statement of opinion ended.

~ "I wonder what color hair will my baby have" she said. "My friend has dark hair."

~ "Will you marry him anyway?" I inquired.

~ "Perhaps. But first, I want to have my baby."

My eyes were weary from the day. I wanted to close them and think about the drive on the Beltway, Route 29 South, and then getting home. I had been on the road for many days this month. I was in the air on the first day of fall. I missed the opening of the first mum bud next to our mailbox. I am sure I also missed many other events in my family.

Being on planes so frequently teaches patience to even the most impulsive of us. Between numerous flights, I believe that one's body changes shape. Now, I fit in all airline seats as if the seat were my own; seats that have absorbed the contours of my anatomy over years. Funny. Perhaps there are many people with my body shape, I once wondered. They compress the seat's foam in ways that my body finds comfortable and rests. As for my legs, the situation in quite different! Not only I couldn't raise them above my heart, I was unable of moving them at all. I think the solution is in letting both of your legs go to sleep. I once explained my theory to a flight attendant (I think Suz was her name.)

~ "If all people learn to let their legs go to sleep, there will be no waiting time at the lavatories. You will not need to change rows when serving the complementary tasteless coffee because someone is returning to their seat. People in Aisle seats do not have to get up twice during a 750 mile trip to accommodate the bladder fantasies of window passengers. Life can be so much easier if people let their legs go to sleep!"

Suz found my thoughts funny. She even put her hand on my right shoulder and said: "I have never heard such a thing!" But, flight attendants find all passengers' thoughts funny. That is part of their training in nice manners, I believe.

~ "I think I am going to get sick" I heard.

~ "Here, the puke-bag."

~ "I ate too much. I can hardly keep a few bites down."

~ "You need to go to the bathroom?"

~ "No. I will try some crackers first."

And like magic, the good old crackers did the trick.

~ "These are life savers" she said, "Do you know why they work so well?"

~ "No idea. As long as they work, you do not need a scientific explanation."

She seemed to recover very well from her malaise.

~ "Do you know what is the temperature in Baltimore?"

~ "Well, this morning when I took my dog out, it was about 42 degrees. I expect a similar temperature tonight. This is the first day of fall, you know."

~ "Yes. This summer was crazy. I was in Shaboygan some time ago, and the water temperature was quite pleasant. Usually it is very cold, the water around Shaboygan. I even tried to swim. I was cold, but bearable. Do you swim in the Chesapeake?"

~ "No, too many jelly fish. I like to go fishing with my friend, but didn't do much of that either, this summer."

~ "I grew up on a farm. We had all kinds of animals, I saw them mate, I saw my father butcher many of them. But never went fishing. Where I come from it is a man's thing, to go fishing."

~ "You should try that" I said, "perhaps even wear your pool shooting apparel to drive the guys crazy!"

~ "Wouldn't that be fun?"

We both laughed. I noticed she had perfectly aligned and perfectly white teeth. Could she convince me that it was her part Swede part German....?

~ "In preparation for landing...."

~ "There, Baltimore at night! It is a beautiful city."

~ "Yes, there is much to this area of the country. It takes time to discover them all. I hope you will stay for some time?"

~ "About a week. Of course, it depends on how my friend is doing. I am really excited about seeing him. It has been more than two weeks since we saw each other last."

~ "I hope your stay is adventuresome" I said.

~ "Don't worry. I am only 8 weeks' pregnant. I can still do a lot with my friend."

The plane landed at the Baltimore-Washington International Airport as smoothly as it had taken off from St. Louis. The time was 8:36 p.m. and I knew much about a 26 years old woman from Bismarck, North Dakota.

~ "It was really nice talking to you" she said.

~ "Same here. Take care of yourself." The airport was quiet. Few faces returning from a long business day travel, others waiting the change of planes. Many rushed to the "Smoking Permitted" section.

I walked gingerly, and realized that she was next to me.

~ "I can't wait to see him" she said. "He told me to go to the lower level."

~ "Yes, the escalators are right there. Good luck."

On my way out of the airport I remembered promising my wife Chinese food for dinner. Or was it Korean? Knowing her Irish temper well, I decided to call for instructions. I looked for a public telephone and realized there was one under the stairs, on the lower level. As I descended, I saw my trip companion rushing toward the luggage area. I followed, almost instinctively. It was my turn to be nosy, and it felt alright.

She walked toward a dark hair, handsome fellow. "The lucky pilot" I thought. She opened her arms wide, but to my surprise, reached the older, very German-Swedish looking man behind the presumed pilot. "Daddy" I heard "so good to see you!"

—October 1, 1992

Screwball

I was on a late night flight, out of Chicago. The day had gone well, and the research findings were promising. After all, a university-based research team was able to demonstrate that... But my mind seemed empty, the kind of state where only the past survives. For it does not need to change; for it has already been.

I had two glasses of red wine with dinner. Pulled the blanket up to my chin, and remembered Chalo. She was my girl, my friend. She was ten years of my life, at least a daily part of it. I pulled the blanket higher. And had the following dream.

~ "Go sweet girl, go."

Chalo looked at him with her brown eyes. She had looked at him day and night, throughout the country, in deep woods, the Grand Canyon, and in bed. She looked at him again. It was a loving look, one that says "I'll do anything for you."

~ "Can I have the leash? And the collar?"

The veterinarian was in tears, he was not. He had watched her sleep that earthly sleep for a decade. Now, she was doing the same thing for a bit longer.

The collar was still warm. He held it tight as if to keep the last warmth within himself. He signed the papers for donating the body to research, paid for the euthanasia, and told the clinic staff that he will be fine. They were very attached to Chalo; she was the mostly-yellow-lab with a smile for everyone.

His mornings were now lonely; he would not go out for his walk or run. He drank a lot of coffee. But he mostly cried. He cried the entire night when he brought Chalo's collar home; he cried every evening after that day for a month. He knew she was gone, and that made him cry. But he also cried for the good times they have had, the three of them. From the cave in Dearborn where they found her to the Rockies, the Grand Tetons, the valleys of Utah, the Great lakes, the Finger Lakes, the Chesapeake Bay, the Hopi Mesas, the Black Forests of Dakota, the backwaters of the Mighty Mississippi. Chalo was the companion, the camper, the baby.

Yes, they lost a baby. He seemed to be much more affected by that loss. Perhaps nor so; his wife was just playing the tough one. He could not care being tough, never did.

And then, an afternoon in August, he brought home a ten weeks old puppy. "The mother is a Chesapeake retriever, a chocolate one" he told his wife. "See, she has her mother's yellow-green eyes."

They called her Pita, for no good reason. She loved licking people's ears. She was very small, thin and long. He was not sure if there was enough Lab in her. The veterinarian was very happy to see that he had a new friend. "You have big paws to fill" he said, "Chalo was the sweetest, of course."

He had saved Chalo's life by operating on both of her hind knees. A hereditary weakness, of sorts. The anterior cruciate ligaments had ruptured during exercise and, given her large size, all feared that the knees will never hold. He tried an experimental reconstructive method, and it worked.

Actually, it worked very well. Chalo chased rabbits and other rodent nuisances for almost 6 years after the surgeries. She was stiff afterwards, as she was after a long rainy day, but who cares? An aspirin tablet, a good night's rest on our firm king size bed, and, Chalo the dog was ready to chase more rabbits.

~ "How much Lab is in Pita?" He asked the vet.

~ "Quite a bit, except the ears. Perhaps the snout is also too long. Hard to tell at ten weeks. But she is loving and funny. Look at those eyes! A screwball!! That's what she is."

And Screwball remained her nickname.

Pita grew up to be a wonderful dog. She was a bit squeamish, had these green-yellow eyes giving her a homy look, and never got to be too big a dog. But she was the most gentle dog either he or his wife had ever had. Pita was a delight, a quiet, loving, dry-mouth, short-coat screwball! She slept on the bed, just like Chalo did, but in a different way. While Chalo slept at the end of the bed, horizontally stretched most of the time, Pita slept next to his wife. "Better there than here," he said, "I will not get up at night coughing hair balls, anymore!"

And, in November of the following year, the family was increased with the arrival of twins, a boy and a girl. "How will Pita take this new change?" they wondered.

Pita bonded with the little ones immediately. She was there next to them when they woke up at night, and when they slept through the night. Later, she was sitting next to their swings and

31

licking their faces as they swung by. He was worried that she might hurt their delicate skins, but Pita knew better. While she could crush and pulverize a lamb's femur, she hardly touched the little ones.

When they started walking, there they were, on top of Pita, pulling her hair, riding her like a pony. And she loved it. "We have triplets" he used to say. And indeed, they played with each other for hours, without either party being physically hurt.

But sometimes, when the twins were too active and demanding, Pita would delicately leave the room and find peace in a vacant bedroom, or on the deck. After all, Pita was six years old, and had lost some of the puppy energy she once had.

~ "Flight 247 went down in the woods, near Emittsburg. There seems to be no survivors."

He was on that flight. He was coming back from a day trip, a business trip. He hated to call his lecturing sessions "business trips." It was more of a conceptual communication session, a fun-filled day of sharing ideas and planning for the next sessions. Well, it was all over now.

The twins were eleven years old. They cried, but really did not know what death was. They had lost a goldfish; butterflies in a box they fed sugar-water; he had gone fishing with his daddy once and seen fish gasping for air at the bottom of the canoe. But it was not enough.

She cried for awhile. Then remarried, as he had always asked her to do. "It will be good for you, and good for the kids. Don't take it as a joke, you may need to face it one day." And he was right. She felt very comfortable marrying a man of her age, a professional who treated her and the twins well.

Pita got the short end of the stick. He did not care much for her. He liked big, strong, pure-blooded dogs. He wanted to feel proud of his dog in public. Pita was a mutt, a screwball! She was as loving as ever, but no one seemed to want her love. Except for the twins. They often played with her, but they were of an age when they learn to be cruel, without meaning so. And Pita was left out there, on her chain, all day long. At night, she slept in the living room, on the cedar-filled bed of her's.

The hips were bothering her. The cold dirt was too harsh on her. She watched the squirrels run in front of her without feeling the urge to scare them away. Pita was 10 years old.

32

She spent long days under the sun, in summer and in the house when it was raining. She had her warm bed, could look out of the window, and sleep most of the time. On cold days, no matter where she was, her hips hurt.

It was a warm August day, 10 years since the day when he had picked her up out of the litter, on a farm in Maryland. She had spent all day under the sun, and was feeling good about life.

Suddenly, she raised her snout into the air, and sucked the air into her pink nostrils. She knew that smell.

She opened her eyes, and sucked the air in again. Yes, it was an old smell, one she would never forget.

Pita looked into the sun. There, she could see him. He was back! She had waited for him for more than five years.

Her hips felt stronger, the pain was gone. The hump on her back disappeared, and she sat down on her back legs, with a straight head on her shoulders. Like the old days.

He walked to her. He had a dog on his side! A big, yellow lab, with a big smile!

Pita sucked more air into her nostrils. She had smelled that dog's smell in the basement, many years ago. And under the daffodil bushes, and near the feeble stream.

He walked to her, gently. Caressed her head, kissed her lips, as he used to do. "How have you been, Pita dog?"

Then, in a very calm voice said, "Pita, meet Chalo."

And the three of them walked together, a man and his dogs, toward the sun.

~ "Baltimore in 10 minutes, please prepare the cabin for landing."

~ "Hi there neighbor,'" my next-seat-companion said, "had a good nap?"

I looked at him with wide open eyes.

~ "That was really bad red wine" I replied.

—*July, 1992*

Rahman the Farsi

I didn't trust him. Or perhaps I was not sure how to react.

~ "That's just too much" I said, "forty-six dollars for a ride to the hotel?"

It was a lovely evening over Kansas city. The last rays were hardly warm, but of a Midwestern brightness they were.

~ "Ok" he said "forty dollars. Then I go home."

I still didn't trust him. My neck extended inward through his cab window, I saw a large and colorful book on the front passenger seat. There was also a melon, the familiar aroma of which was anachronistic but soothing.

~ "Isn't there another way for getting to the hotel?"

~ "Sure, you can wait for the shuttle. The 40 miles could take more then an hour to make. See on this map, that is where you are going."

It was the first time a cab driver had shown to me the location of the major area hotel on a map! What was the alternative? There were no other hotels where I was going. Was he trying to lure me into something? I did not trust the process; one should not have to see the location of the Overland Marriott on a map.

I was tired. I looked back and through the freshly cleaned back window saw another cab coming. I stopped it. A young man, very middle-eastern looking, exited the cab. I shared with him my skepticism.

~ "He is a good man" he replied, "he wouldn't lie or cheat. He made you a very good offer. Take it."

The older gentleman, the first cab driver, had joined us. He listened to the praise with no noticeable expression. He was obviously upset that I did not trust him. He was murmuring in a language I might have known.

What a funny situation! There I was, after a long day in the air, at the junction of three states, at the International Airport of Kansas City. I was not in any mood to bargain, nor that there was any competition to bargain for! (Anyone who has been to KCI airport on an October evening knows what I'm talking about.) It was just bloody too much to pay for a ride to the only major city in town.

Realizing that my choices were few, I jumped into the first cab and felt how comfortable the old Chevy seats were.

For a few miles, we were silent. I looked at him really for the first time. Probably from Afghanistan, I thought. The skin color, the prominence of the nose, the long fingers, and the type of dental work he had on his incisive reminded me of the people from Pakistan or perhaps India. He was wearing a blue baseball cap and kept on pronouncing the "W" as a "V" and the "V" as a "W."

He was in his 50's, and in apparent good physical shape. When he talked, he had hand and neck movements that seemed at a different tempo from the usual. It was a strange feeling. I thought I was in the middle of an MTV video. The car speed seemed to change with his own neck movements: the vast, open space was bathing in the day's final rays, and the air seemed still. Funny, for a few moments, all was quiet and moving at a quarter metronome beat too slow...

~ "The rain has stopped" he started "we had many of those days. Not nice."
(I realized that he also pronounced "nice" in a peculiar way. It was more like "nayyss!".)

~ "I was in Lawrence last week" I said, "and many fields were still wet and muddy. The soil is certainly saturated with water."

~ "The great food of 1993!" he qualified, raising his chin high and waving his long index in the air.

~ "I will show you the damage to the road" he promised.
He seemed a pleasant man.

~ "How far is the hotel?"

~ "Thirty eight miles and a block" he said, "you didn't trust me. I told you it was far."
He was hurt.

~ "It is a lot of money, I know" he continued.

"It is not that I didn't trust you" I said, "I was just surprised. I usually rent a car or someone picks me up."

~ "I know" and he smiled.

I was curious about the book. Listening to him describe the great flood of 1993, the situation on the roads, the misery of the people, I felt comfortable with the situation. I had seen numerous

TV news sequences about the flood, and his description did fit the images I had seen. But, partly attracted by the aroma of the melon, I was increasingly leaning forward, placing my forearms on the back of the front seat. I was mostly curious about the book.

Although the title was written in Arabic letters, I couldn't interpret the words.

~ "In what language is this book written?"

~ "Farsi" he said, without surprise and his eyes glued to the road.

~ "So, you are from Iran?"

~ "Yes."

~ "I am Armenian" I said, knowing that most Iranians have had an Armenian acquaintance sometime in their lives.

"Armeni? There are a lot of Armenis in Tehran" he happily replied, "most of them professionals. Very nayyss!"

I took the book and started reading. I was reading words phonetically through the Arabic alphabet. Only a few words sounded familiar. He was correcting my pronunciation. I could make sense only by mentally searching for analogies between Arabic and Turkish words and my phonetically pronounced Farsi. The murmur of the car and the vastness of the corn fields created the perfect atmosphere for learning a new language, I thought.

It was a children's book. Sort of an encyclopedia where Gaugin, Van Gogh, the geography of France, and maritime electric cable installation methods were presented.

~ "How come you know Arabic?" he asked.

~ "I was born in Lebanon."

~ "Lubnan? Very nayyss!"

Everything was nayyss: The hotel where I was going, the orange fields of Lubnan, the...

The Armenian in me was boiling; I had to ask him about a historic Armenian lake, now located within the geopolitical boundaries of Iran.

~ "Do you know lake Van?"

He didn't. But as I was describing it, he recognized it as lake Urmiya. That was its name now. He explained to me that during the Pahlavi dynasty, the Shah had renamed it in his own name. Now it was Urmya again.

~ "I have been there. There is a church, I think, an Armeni church."

I was inclined not to believe him. But, why not? Perhaps he has really been there. After all, my initial reaction to this man has been overly and overtly unnecessary.

I was about to inquire further about lake Van, when he continued.

~ "I have also been to Kharakilless. There are many Armenis there. Do you know the story?"

~ "Yes."

~ "It was during the reign of Shah Abbas" he continued without paying much attention to my response "he was a very powerful and wise man. He brought hoards of Armenys to Persia and especially to Tabriz. He gave them all the respect and freedom. They, in turn, gave Persia art and science. They also became model citizens. That was 600 years ago. There is another very nayyss Armeni Gregory church in Tabriz. There are a lot of books there."

I was surprised to find an Iranian recanting my people's history on a Kansas highway, which was flooded a few weeks ago. It seemed unreal, out of place, time and sequence. The last rays were still shining on the fields. The Chevy was racing to that 'thirty eight miles and a block' away very nayyss hotel.

~ "All Armenis in Tehran are Gregori" he said, "are you?"

~ "Yes, I am Gregorian. It is from Saint Gregory, the Patron of the Armenian Orthodox church."

I asked him if there are mosques in Kansas city. There were three mosques and a lot of worshipers.

~ "But the Muzzeddine is not there" he said referring to the clerical who calls the worshiper's to pray from the mosques' minaret. "Imagine the people of Kansas city waking up at the call of the Muzeddine!...."

(That would be something to see, I thought, at the very early hours of the day, and five times a day.)

I was still interested in knowing why he had a children's book with him. And, a melon...

"Oh, I never had the opportunity to read books when I was young," he said, "I worked with my hands. Now, I discover how much I have missed. I do not want to miss more."

I noticed that the book was published in 1978. That much I could read; the numerical annotation is the same in Farsi and in Arabic. But didn't share my thoughts with him. After all, the work and lives of Gaugin and Van Gogh will not change between a 1978 and 1993 publication. Perhaps the locomotive technology did, but....

~ "I read between two customers" he said. "Sometimes, I have a lot of time to read!"

I smiled. Yes, things are not always intense, in Kansas City.

~ "Lubnan was beautiful, no?"

~ "Yes. It was a piece of heaven that fell near the Mediterranean" I replied borrowing from an old Lebanese song.

~ "Did you have pomegranate, in Lubnan?"

Strange question. It took me a second to change gears.

~ "Big ones too" I said. "Juicy, sweet, with the aroma of the sun condensed in each fruitlet. It invaded your mouth and soul at every bite."

I suddenly realized that in the space of a few minutes I was speaking Arabic through the English language! It felt good. He was at ease with that image and metaphor adoring language, and I was that young man again, somewhere around the bluest of all seas.

~ "We had the best pomegranates" he said stressing the "we." "There was a tree in the front of our home. I used to climb and pick those huge, red, juicy wonders. I would give anything to eat one of these again!"

~ "I used to do the same with black fig trees" I counter-attacked. "The figs would be soaking the sun, would be warm. I would sometimes wait till that very moment when the skin cracks and the nectar oozes. Then, I would pick it, smell it, put it in my mouth, with my tongue pressure it onto the roof of my mouth, and slowly become invaded with the taste of that fig."

~ "By God, that sounds even better then my pomegranates!"

We laughed. By then, I trusted the man who was driving an old Chevy in Kansas City.

~ "What is your name?"

~ "Rahman, in God's name. And yours?"

~ "Vahé."

38

~ "Wahed?"

I said yes. That has happened with me so often that it does not bother me anymore. I think that other then my family and childhood friends, only my wife pronounces my name correctly. And even she, sometimes...

~ "Oh" he happily announced "Wahed is God's name too! It means 'one' you know? Only God is one."

Yes, only God the Merciful is one.

~ "Is your wife a good woman?"

Jumping from one topic to another was perhaps his way of keeping customers alert on these monotonous roads. Especially when the topics were profoundly personal. I realized that in the hundreds of encounters with cab drivers over the years, no one has ever asked me such a question. They usually ask about my job, and we find some common ground for small talk. This man was different.

~ "Yes, she is a good woman."

~ "Good. That is very important. I have two Iranian friends here" he said, " one has a very nayyss wife, but the other....!"

And he threw his arms up.

~ "She destroyed the poor man. It is very important to have a good wife."

~ "Nassib" I said hoping that the word for "destiny" was the same in Farsi, Arabic and Turkish.

~ "Nassib and Kismet!" he replied, happy that I knew so many things from his culture.

We stopped in front of the Marriott.

~ "I am very happy about this trip" he said. "I have never had a customer with whom I could discuss so many things from home."

He shook my hand, and gave me his card.

~ "Call me next time you're here."

~ "I will. Salam Aleykum for now."

While entering the hotel, I realized that I had not asked Rahman about the melon on the front seat. I smiled. Well, I'll do that on my next trip to Kansas City....

—*September 30, 1993*

Diana

She was a small woman. Perhaps Italian. Her eyes were bloodshed and she was crying in secret.

We were in line waiting for the airline news.

~ "Delayed till 7 p.m. Sorry folks, the President's visit altered all plans. Stay close to this area, we will board as soon as possible".

Columbus Day week end, Newark airport. It was supposed to be a simple one day trip, two presentations to medical staffs of two local hospitals and an early flight back to Baltimore. But, President Clinton decided to speak to the same group of physicians with whom I was scheduled to meet. He brought Air force One to Newark, and stopped traffic for two hours. Things moved again at five o'clock but the back-up load was too much for Newark, on the eve of a holiday week end.

~ "It is not what people think it is" I said to her. "Travel is really getting to be a hassle."

She smiled. She had an attractive smile. Specially through her bloodshed eyes. She was hardly older than a mature teenager. Perhaps mid twenties, I thought.

~ "My boyfriend is waiting for me in Baltimore. We have tickets to the hockey game."

~ "You like hockey?"

~ "Not really. I love my boyfriend."

Honest answer. After all, don't we all go grocery shopping?

I was hoping we would get out of Newark before eight o'clock. So, I proposed to get out of the line and watch the planes take off.

~ "It reminds me of my childhood" I said, "watching these metal cigars take off and disappear. Sort of a funny dream where things that should not fly find a way to do so, eventually".

Another middle aged man followed us. He was ready for small talk.

~ "Things always happen this way" he said, "it is part of the fun of travel."

And then, he proposed to share with us a chocolate bar. Great, it was really like in the old days when I used to have a candy bar while watching planes take off from the Beirut International Airport.

Gosh, that was many moons ago, and since, I have probably been on a thousand flight, all over the
globe. I realized, though, that the initial excitement was not there, although the chocolate tasted really good.

~ "Can I leave my stuff with you for a sec? I will try to call Baltimore."

Sure, we were going no where. We, the two middle aged man, on a business trip to Newark.

~ "Do you come to Newark often?" The question was expected. That is the best way to break the ice in an airport, or a lonely bar somewhere near Penn Station.

~ "Not really. I have made this trip a few times in the past two years."

~ "It is usually not too bad. But today the President...."

~ "Yeah. He spoke to the same group I was supposed to speak. Not only he changed my schedule, but also those of thousands in this area."

~ "You are in healthcare?"

So we talked about some petty experiences with hospitals and illness. He was a pleasant man, one that will never leave any lasting memories in one's mind. He was the every day traveler you meet in airports between two flights, or in the bar having a beer, watching Oprah.

~ "He is not there" said the young woman. "I have not his beeper's number with me. I usually do. Of course, not this time!"

She was wearing a slightly oversized pullover. Her hair was shiny, curly, and dark, although it was clear that the wait and humidity in the airport were taking a toll on its luster. She exhibited a somewhat sophisticated simplicity. It was perhaps the lack of make up. Or perhaps, it was the disappointment of missing the hockey game that she handled pretty well.

~ "All flights are canceled. Sorry, folks, nothing we can do. Blame it on the President."

It was one of these moments when the business travel takes on a totally new turn. I had been there many times. I never accepted it, though. But not much choice, I had to get back to Baltimore. My wife was giving a party next day, and my assignments were clear:

41

bathrooms, bathing the dog, and preparing the burgers. I could not stay in Newark tonight.

I called her. She said it was a lovely evening in Columbia. They just came back from a long walk, and that the pooch was happy. She was getting ready for a pasta dish with garlic and olive oil, pine nuts, sun dried tomatoes, and fresh oregano from the garden. I could smell the garlic in oil. I always felt that garlic and olive oil made our house a home.

~ "My daughter is a medical student" our companion, the middle-aged man said. "She wants to become a D.O. She is vegetarian, you know. How different is a D.O.'s training from an M.D.?"

~ "My father is a D.O." the young woman with a friend in Baltimore replied. "He loves it."

I knew more about her, now.

~ "Well, I am going back to Maryland" I told her, "either by train or by renting a car. What are your plans?"

I was feeling young that night. When wearing a suit, I often do not live my age. There are certain things I do, others that I fancy about. I never ask for tomato juice on my flight in, for example. Once, I saw a gentleman's suit and white shirt ruined by an air pocket. I also do not exchange business cards with my temporary travel companions. A nurse I met on a flight to St. Louis called my back once, when on a trip to Baltimore. I find the hassle unnecessary. But, that night, on the eve of Columbus Day week end, I felt like I should do what I felt like doing: behave like a college kid on his way home.

~ "I do not know what to do! It is silly to stay here, no? I think I will get the train myself."

It was alright. Having an unknown young woman accept to travel with me made me feel comfortable. We decided to rent a cab and catch the first train out of Newark's Penn Station.

"Wait a minute" I realized. "We should get our ticket's fee reimbursed. It is really not our fault...."

So we ran to the airline counter. I helped her with her bags. They were heavy, well-traveled and awkwardly shaped. It was clear that she had stuffed them, perhaps at the last minute.

42

She was not much of an athlete, I noticed. She was running awkward, like someone running out of a house on fire while still in deep sleep. There was no natural rhythm to her jog. I wished there were. The awkwardness of her cadence did not seem to match well with the youthfulness she emanated.

Of course, the reimbursement was on another floor, in a different wing. When we got there, we realized that dozens of other passengers had the same idea before us.

Finally our turn came, but by then the pneumatic system was broken. Communication between the station and the money source was cut. A caring employee looked at my companion's face, tired and crying eyes and decided to help us. I think there is always one such soul in every airport.

But the time was getting dangerously close to the 9:30 p.m. scheduled train to Baltimore. We finally got our money in cash, and ran out for a taxi.

Needless to say, we were again in line.

~ "We will never make it" she said. "This is unbelievable."

~ "Health care reform is not easy" I tried to joke, "you know, the President spoke of personal responsibility. You are exercising it right now!"

She looked at me with her brown eyes. (Her eyes were just that-brown. Not a touch of honey, or the shiny darkness of umber.) She did not find it funny, and made her thoughts abundantly clear. It was comforting to see her react that way. It meant that she was feeling better. Perhaps even comfortable with me, I fancied.

~ "No problem" the very Middle Eastern cab driver said, "we will get to train station in less then 12 minutes."

Cab drivers have a subtle way of comforting, I find. They use highly specific language like "a block and three quarters away", "38 miles and a block from here", and "we will be there in about 11 minutes". Even when I know the statement to be questionable, I find it possible that they know something I don't.

And he did. We were at the station in less then 10 minutes.

~ "The train is delayed! Now what?"

She was obviously upset.

~ "Let's have something to eat" I said. "I have not had dinner yet. Have you?"

~ "That sounds good. I saw a bakery at the entrance of the station."

The Station Bakery, was a lonely place with a few stale pastries, banana-nut muffins, and giant soft pretzels. The employees were tired, the white polyester make-believe baker attires in desperate need for a permanent press cycle with bleach. They wore bakers head pieces, too. At the end of a long day, the banana-nut muffins and the employees had the same look: fixtures of the Bakery that had unattractive growths on top. The employees were not much interested in the customers. When I asked for two non-salt pretzels, she didn't even look at me. She just stuffed the small microwave with two bags, ran it on high for a few seconds and handed the warm, giant, unsalted pretzels to me. During that time, I was thinking about my wife's dinner--fresh pasta, virgin olive oil, large cloves of garlic browning in it, and the aroma of dried red Roma tomatoes sauteed in that heavenly mixture. That evening, my share was a freshly zapped pretzel, that was probably made a few months ago in a South West Chicago warehouse.

....We ate our soft, giant and stale pretzels in silence. We were busy watching the hundreds of people around us. It was a cold night, and a number of homeless people had found refuge in the warm station. Many of them were sleeping on the large wooden benches. There was one who was snoring loud enough that even with the brouhaha of all around us, we could participate in the cadenced draw of his laryngeal vibrations.

The pretzels were history. We disposed off the wrappers and the numerous little) mustard bags we used to enhance our dinner's taste. I had noticed a men's room, next to the bakery.

~ "Be back in a minute, don't leave without me" I joked.

She seemed in a better mood. Her eyes were sparkling while she combed her hair. Perhaps she was hungry, that's all, I thought.

I was the only one wearing a suit and a tie. Upon entry to the mens room, I saw two young men on the floor, needles in their arms. A third person was shaving, and a fourth drying his chest and neck under the air blowing contraption. He had obviously had an improvised sponge bath few minutes ago.

I left the urinal quickly, without even flushing, I think. It was an uncomfortable situation. The last time I saw people shooting stuff in their arms was an early morning in Detroit airport. In no other public facility I have seen such display of total independence of act and posture.

On my way out I saw a policeman, with all the gear, and black, cut-off-finger gloves. His chest was bulging and his waist was small. He looked like he had just finished pumping iron at the gym. He stopped at the men's room door and looked around. A few seconds later, left.

I wanted to say something, perhaps even tell him about his job. But I didn't. He had large shoulders and I had a ticket for Baltimore.

We finally got into the train, and found two seats, one on each side of the aisle. We were tired, but happy to be able to sleep in our own beds, tonight.

~ "Let me find the bar" I said, "it is grand time for a beer. Interested?"

Sure, she was. A beer would put her to sleep, she said, and that was fine by her.

I bought the last two bottles of beer, and two small bottles of Merlot. One should never travel without some wine, I thought. Upon return, I found a young woman in the seat next to mine.

~ "Hi" I said.

We drank the beer, and things looked better. We did not talk much. The night wagon was comfortable and the monotonous train rhythm, soothing. I realized that I had not taken a train for a number of years. I used to travel to Montreal frequently from Windsor, Ontario when a student in Ann Arbor, Michigan. Since, life has been on the fast track, or rather in the air, most of the time.

~ "Staying in Baltimore?" I asked my new travel companion.

~ "No. Visiting my mother, in Frederick."

She had a very distinct southern French accent.

~ "Francaise?" did I reply in French.

~ "Oui. You obviously speak French."

Sure, French was a language I grew up with. France is the country where my family resides.

~ "Can I offer you some wine? I have a one-glasser."

~ "I have better then that. Here, would you like some Scotch? Its a twelve year young bottle."

Do I like Scotch! Is there sand in the Arabian desert?

So we toasted to the French. And why not? It had been a long day.

~ "You always travel with a bottle of Scotch?"

~ "No. I was taking it as a present to my mother. But the day was long, and I decided to test it first."

She was very young. Perhaps 24 years old. She way sort of boyish. Boyish with long, blond hair. She also seemed very athletic. It is hard not to notice large shoulders on a woman.

She was a first year medical student at Boston U. Great, now I have another person to talk to, especially about a topic I knew.

~ "You know French songs?"

Sure, but the last song I heard was probably 12 or 13 years ago. Things had changed since, specially for her generation.

~ "Lets play a game" she said. "I will start a song and see if you can continue."

I looked over my left shoulder, and my travel companion had shut her eyes. The beer really worked well on her.

~ "Ok. But try to remember songs from your childhood. That is probably where my acquaintance stops."

But it did not. To my surprise, she was still singing many of the songs I used to, as a young man. "These are classics" she said. The atmosphere in the wagon got increasingly quiet. Most passengers were sleeping. It was past midnight, somewhere between Newark and Baltimore.

But we were singing. The twelve year old Scotch does wonders on the tired mind and body.

"Ca fait long temps que je t'aime.."

"..Jamais je ne t'oublierai"

"Les roses de la Picardie.."

"Quand il me prends dans ses bras.."

"et murmure tout bas.."

"je vois la vie on ro-o-se..!"

It was unreal, it was childish, it felt wonderful!
~ "Baltimore, Penn Station is next!"
I woke my sleeping companion up.
~ "You made it! I hope the hockey game was a bore."
She smiled. Her half asleep eyes were charming.
~ "Thanks for your help. I couldn't have made this trip alone."
~ "Oh yes you could. No problem."
I helped her with her luggage. And suddenly realized that I did not know her name!

~ "By the way, what's your name?"
She laughed.
~ "I thought you would never ask. Diana."
~ "I am Vahé. Nice to have met you."
~ "Same here. Take care."
The train moved again. Next was the B.W.I. stop. I looked to my next-seat companion and started a new song.

I have taken many trips since, but keep a warm smile for Diana. She was the most ordinary young woman, who accepted to share a train ride with me from Newark to Baltimore. I hardly new her name, or anything much about her. But in the space of about four hours, I untied my tie, talked about simple things, and felt wonderfully young, again. I realized that feeling good on a trip back from a business day, was important.

—*Columbus Day, 1995*

Meet Me in St. Louis, Erin

~ "My pleasure" I said hanging up the phone, "I'll see you in St. Louis."

I had stopped being on the lecture circuit; my life was now filled by and dedicated to our twins, a boy and a girl. Gifts from the heavens. And also, I was getting older. Travel has long lost its glamour; the lonesome hotel rooms and delayed flights have taken a toll on me. After nearly 15 years of crisscrossing the United States and many parts of our shrinking planet, I decided to stay home and smoke my pipe. Like an ancestor. Like an aging son.

So I did.

But sometimes, for whatever reason, I did not have the quickness, I guess, of saying no. So, it turned out to be a yes. St. Louis was one of them.

I left Baltimore on a pleasant August afternoon to arrive in St. Louis on a steamy evening. It was hot, like the South knows; enough to cook crawdads in their own mud, in the backwaters of the mighty Mississippi. I was in Mark Twain's territory , and it was time to share the ride with his characters in mind.

I had been to St. Louis many times. It is everything people have said to be. But, for a short trip, it can be lonely. To food is plenty, but no matter how often I've tried , I've never been able to consume more than three meals in one afternoon. And then what? There are 6 more hours to sacrifice on the altar of the lecture circuit. So, I plan to write, on trips to St. Louis. Write about other places, write about other people. I have written some of my most cherished poems and stories during trips to the Mid West and the South; the space is vast, I guess, and the fields are to dreams.

I hired a cab. Too hot to wait for the free shuttle. The asphalt and concrete surroundings were baking in the afternoon sun; I could see well dressed ladies transpire profusely, and me draw on their cigarettes to burn their throats in despair.

A young man from Africa was my driver. Wearing the stereotypical black pants and white shirt of drivers, he has a handkerchief rolled as a scarf, around his neck. Perhaps as a fashion statement, but surely to minimize the wetness of his shirt. I could see traces of salty patches on his shirt, a sign that he has been sweating since early that day. Or that he was saving money by minimizing his laundry bills. "Yes Sir" he said, "next to the Ramada. About six dollars." He stressed the "R" of the Ramada in a prominent way, like a badly tuned motorcycle, like one who does not roll his "R"s. Like a tired cab driver on a hot afternoon in St. Louis.

My room was a non-smoking room, with a heavy smoke smell. Strange. Many hotel rooms I have found to be that way. I think they alter the room's status according to demand. Now smoking, tomorrow not. The feeling is a funny one, when you enter such a room. You don't know if it will make you sick or just tease you. Or angry. A non-smoking room where people before you have smoked is like a Thursday night date who leaves around midnight: you wake up alone on Friday morning.

It did not bother me much. Pushed the thermostat regulating arm all the way down to 40 degrees and took a shower. For some strange reason, while in the warm water was running down my back, I thought about the woman at the window seat, Aisle 14. It was a few hours ago, on my trip down to St. Louis. She was a large woman wearing tight shorts and sandals. Perhaps early 30's. I was in seat 14D, she was in 14A. She said "Hi" and I smiled. My mind was on the paper I was trying to finish writing. I had promised Laura, my assistant, to Fax a few pages to her from the hotel, upon arrival. Which I did. But during the 1 hour and 57 minutes flight at 35 thousand feet, I sometimes looked at her, at her legs. Could not understand why she was wearing these tight shorts. They did not make her legs look thinner. But there was something more about her, something I did not realize till we touched down in St. Louis. "Well, a successful one!" I said. "Are you Iranian?" she replied. Strange, I thought. "No, Armenian, sort of northern neighbors to XerXes's nephews." She smiled. "I had Armenian friends in Tehran." Small world. And what a change in dress code!

The shower was refreshing, and my Iranian acquaintance soon fled my mind. I realized that there was nothing interesting in the room. Two large TV sets, a writing desk, a loud air conditioning system, one bar of soap, a shower cap, towels that smelled cigarette smoke, and a big sign on the door: "This is a non-smoking room." Yeah, and I was Iranian!

Oh well, I decided to go for a walk, to change the scenery. "Walking distance?" the front desk clerk replied, "Well, you can walk to the Ramada. It is half a block away." Walking from the Embassy Suites to the Ramada! What a prospect, in St. Louis!

I did. But first called home, told my wife I miss her, and that the daily exhaustion from raising twins was better than the calm, the boring calm. I asked about the dog. "She misses you, you know that," she replied. Yeah, she is a good pooch. Our baby before the twins. She still sleeps on our bed.

Then left for the Ramada. It is like any other Ramada, predictable, un-personable, and clean. "Glenlivet, on a few rocks." In her thirties, wearing the unattractive black tight polyester blend skirt with a generous cleavage on one side, exposing her right thigh. I looked around. The Metal Manufactures were having a conference. I wondered about the issues. I remembered the thrills I used to get, as a young man, from the sight of a thigh, or a pectoral cleavage. I smiled. And holding the single malt nectar up, drank to the old days. Like I would do when remembering a friend from the boy scout days. Or a girlfriend from the abundant days. This time, I drank to myself, the way I remembered me.

Back to the Embassy Suites. People in the lobby recognized me, and said how happy they were I accepted to deliver the key note address for the conference. "It is my pleasure" I said, "It is always pleasant to see known faces." Indeed, it is. But the hiking path from the Embassy Suites to the Ramada?...

It soon was time for dinner. "What are my options of restaurants?" I asked the front desk clerk. "We serve food right there" he said, pointing to the same area where people were having complementary happy hour cocktails, and watching baseball on a big screen.

~ "Yes, sir, ready for dinner?" asked a well groomed and soft spoken black Maître D'.

~ "Can I see the menu?" I asked. "Tonight, we have a salad, pasta with good sauce, and prime rib. You will eat slowly and I am sure you'll enjoy it." "Pasta and prime rib?" I wondered. "Yes, sir. Two great dishes for the price of one!" And, he pointed to the prime rib slab, sitting on a cutting white marble bloc, under a heat lamp. The executioner was a young black woman, wearing well starched white Chef's suit and hat, sharpening her meat knife upon a steel rod, while smiling at me. I was intimidated. I did not say no. Just tried to recall if I ever had stayed in a hotel where the restaurant did not have a menu. "Please, sit anywhere you want," he interrupted

50

my thoughts, "you're the first customer tonight." And, sitting face to the large screen TV, I remained the only customer for at least 45 minutes, when I left. Both the Maître D; and the executioner of ribs waved good bye. I don't think I ate the rib. It was still bleeding in my plate.

I was glad to be back to my room. As I entered, the unappealing smell of tobacco smoke overwhelmed me, but I got used to it in a few seconds. Took my shoes off, and turned the TV on, primarily for background noise. The auditory calm I was experiencing away from the twins, and the pooch, was overwhelming. I felt better with the commercials on the screen.

Without paying attention to the tube, I was going through my slides, rearranging their orders, taking some out. I always try to see if there is a more contemporary contextual interpretation for an old slide. Often, thee is, and an old slide becomes up-to-date again.

Bonanza was on. Who can forget the famous intro music? I looked up. The Virginia map was burning and the Cartwright family was riding through the flames. I realized that I had never seen Bonanza in color. No, 35 years ago, when I watched my first episode on a black and white tube (it was a tube then), it was somewhere in the mountains of Lebanon, in Broummana, I think. There should have been French and Arabic subtitles. No one in our family spoke English.

A few seconds later, there was the title of tonight's episode "ERIN". My God, I thought, that was one of the episodes I remember, from three decades ago! I rationalized the strange parade of the day's events by believing that I needed an oasis of comfort, and ERIN was it.

The story? Simple. Hoss, the ever lovable bear of every child, finds a white Indian lady in the lower plains, and realizes that she needs medical care. He brings her back to the Cartwright ranch, she gets well, and tells how, an Irish woman ended up being raised by Indians. That there is a prophecy on upon her head, and that the Indians think that she has been touched by the gods. Hoss, in his candor and immense goodness, falls in love with Erin. She accepts to become his wife even after saying "Don't be fooled by one good spring day." No, Hoss wanted her by himself, as life's partner. But things turn otherwise. The white folks reject the idea of having Indians become family with the Cartwrights and, in a gun battle overs such noble principle, Erin is killed. Hoss, the bear with tender

51

lips, cries rivers while holding her hand and kissing her lips as if to absorb her last breath.

I was glued to my seat, tears running down my cheeks. I remembered the story, or parts of it, but realized that its interpretation had changed over the years. Now, this was a sad story, one where Hoss had cried, loving an Irish woman. Hoss had defied customs and rules, in his gentle way. But he lost Erin to the prophecy perhaps.

I wiped my eyes with the back of my hand. I watched Bonanza 35 years ago, so did my brother a few years later. Now, in the Embassy Suites of St. Louis, I watched it again. In color this time. The color of injustice. And I cried for the Irish girl who died. Like I cried for my Irish friend who died of cancer last Christmas. And I cried for Hoss, for he brought back my childhood, for a short space.

I was feeling relieved. Things were happening in this hotel, after all! Who would have thought that the past is always with us, that images are imprinted in us for ever, and that they surface in most unlikely ways, in most unlikely places. Like is an Armenian, in St. Louis, a steamy August night.

I needed to celebrate the present state of things. So, I ordered a single malt whiskey (no rocks, please!) to my room. Found a writing pad and a decent pen, put my feet up on the window rim, and wrote about the day. Slowly, between a sip of scotch whiskey and a thought of Erin. The Erins of the world. The Erins I knew.

Tomorrow morning at eight, I will probably mention Erin to a group of clinicians who will think that I have lost touch with epidemiological research. That I had too short a night to gather my thoughts. But while looking at their bewildered faces, I will probably think about the joy of having twins, an Irish wife, and an old dog, back in Maryland. And then, the Embassy Suites in St. Louis will seem a very unique place. Where I realized that Hoss cries, and that there are hotels where restaurants have no menu. Just the catch of the day. Sometimes, that may be a moment of the past.

—*August, 1996*

Lindsay's Mother

That was the day when I decided to avoid lecturing to non-academically inclined audiences. After more than a dozen years of presentations, on that trip to Chicago I realized that in order to be creative one has to feel the audience getting creative while listening. The Chicago audience of that hazy August day in 1995 was not willing to be creative.

It was an important awakening for me. Still under the feeling of the moment, I called my office and asked to cancel my next presentation. "Tell them I am not interested in the topic" I said to my assistant, "I need to think things over." This was a first for me, and Laura was wondering if I felt well. "You sure?" I was. And I took a cab back to O'Hare.

Otherwise, it was an ordinary day. Usual traffic around the Loop, the Hancock Tower lost in the hazy afternoon, and the Ugandan cab driver avid of the vanilla car deodorant. We even had a summer shower to tone down the reckless driving of many.

I had two hours to kill, somewhere between C and D Concourses. Although it was yet early, I thought dinner could fill some of that time. I do not eat well on day trips, and this one was not an exception. The menu was the same on many of my trips to O'Hare: soft pretzel, beer and pistachio ice cream. (It is always a moment of chuckle for the finance department when they receive my expenses from trips to Chicago....) I pulled the most recent copy of the Lancet from my briefcase, and checked the content. A few topics were of immediate interest to me, and I submerged myself into their details. Soon it was time to board the plane.

It was ten o'clock in the evening, and I was looking forward to the easy trip: a few moments of reading, and then the lights go off and all aboard go to sleep. Perhaps that is the single most enjoyable moment on bad day trips , like the one I just experienced.

The plane was ready and we were asked to board. Many were returning from a business day, tired and ready for an hour's nap. One can see the faces, one can feel the moment: the plane is just another box, a transportation means from work to home, or sometimes, to yet another work place. The windows have no meaning since no one looks out; the food has no taste since taste buds are numb; the only saving grace on a late night flight is the reclining aisle seat.

I proceeded to my aisle seat, folded my coat and threw it in the overhead bin. The person next to me was a young woman, and her daughter had the window seat. I smiled. My children are now in bed, I thought, and my wife is probably checking what's on "Larry King live." Or perhaps, she is walking the dog. A short walk, just in the backyard.   I took my shoes off and unfolded the blanket. We should be taking off soon.

~ "Nice tie" she said.

~ "Yeah, one of my favorites."

We took off a few minutes later. I shut my eyes, but felt that she was looking at me.

~ "Going home?"

That is perhaps the most commonly asked first question on a plane ride. Often, it means nothing. Just a pleasantry.

~ "No. This is the cheaper way to going home" she replied. "I live in Pennsylvania."

I don't know why I noticed that she was not wearing a wedding band. It did not surprise me, since many people do not. But often, it seems that men avoid wearing their band. Whatever the reason, women pay more attention to such things.

~ "My husband will pick us up in Baltimore. We then have three hours of drive."

~ "Gosh, you will not be home before three in the morning! I hope your little girl can take a nap."

~ "She will."

I looked at her for the first time. As a frequent traveler, I have developed the unfortunate habit of talking to people next seat without much eye contact. Why not? We will never meet again. It is just a pleasant way of filling idle time. On a lucky day, one may hear a funny story, but that is about it.

~ "She is losing her baby teeth."

~ "Yes, but the new ones will be strong and healthy" I obliged.

She was in her mid twenties, blond hair and blue eyes. I could not tell if she was tall or short. She had french style manicured nails, no make up, a tee-shirt with floral design. Her hair was permed, perhaps very recently. She had a genuine look to herself, sort of wholesome and real.

54

~ "Did you enjoy Chicago?" I asked, using the second most banal ice-breaking question in air travel.

~ "We are coming from Texas" she said, "we have been up since six this morning. It has been a long day."

And without waiting for my next question continued. ~"I was visiting my family for a month. It was fun but I got tired of it. I am ready to go home, although I understand that the weather has been real bad. It was nice in Texas."

~ "Are you a Texan?"

~ "No, I was born in Louisiana, and my brothers in Seattle. My father was a minister, so we've been all over. That is hard, you know, we had to make friends all over again."

~ "But a great experience in early life, I am sure" I replied.

~ "Perhaps. But I am not putting my child through that. By the way, was the weather really that bad, around here?"

Yes, the famous summer of 1995, when Baltimore broke all previous records with thirty two consecutive days of more than ninety degrees heat.

~ "It has been a very bad season for my tomatoes," I said, "hot and dry, they never got the time to enjoy the evening cool and the morning mist. As for my rose bushes, the Japanese beetles did a number on them."

She did not reply, just looked at me with interest, as if awaiting the next conversation line.

~ "Where is home?"

~ "A small town east of Selinsgrove. You probably never heard of it."

~ "Oh yes, I know exactly where that is. Right off Route 15, yes? I drive by it on my way to upstate New York."

~ "Oh? Not many people know about our little town!"

~ "There is always one."

We laughed. She had an attractive smile.

~ "I love your tie" she continued, "my brother is a tie designer in Texas."

I had never known a tie designer.

~ "That should be a fun thing to do. Is that his job?"

~ "One of the things he does. He has a whole closet full of silk ties. It is good that he has to wear a suit . He can use his ties."

~ "He is very good with his hands," she continued, " see, he also did the flowers on my tee-shirt."

~ "Nice job. Have you washed it yet?"

~ "No. But it should be OK, especially if you wash it inside out."

There was a few minutes pause. I was wondering if I should keep to be pleasant or just take a short nap.

~ "Lindsay, shut your eyes," I heard, "we still have a long trip with daddy."

What the heck, I thought, I'll be sleeping in a couple of hours.

~ "What does your husband do?"

~ "He is a supervisor in the only factory in town. Not much choice where we are: it is chickens, farming, or cows. He opted for manufacturing."

I suddenly realized that her attraction was from the down -to - earth, real people character. She had no superfluous mannerism. A young woman from a small Pennsylvania town.

We were almost half way thru the flight time. Lindsay shut her eyes, and seemed to be snoozing. I could hear at least two passengers snoring in the front seats.

~ "You look tired," she said.

~ "I am. I have been up since four thirty this morning."

Without saying more, I pulled my blanket towards my chest and shut my eyes. I had the strange feeling that she did the same.

Here I was, an aging man, returning from a day's work. Thirty three thousand feet in the air, and for the strangest of reasons, I felt like a teenager again! There was this woman next to me, with her eyes shut, and her head leaning toward my left shoulder. I smiled in secret. Big deal! How many times have I had a woman or a man sleep next to me on a flight? Probably hundreds of time. I especially remembered the judge from D.C. who slept on my shoulder, on and off, during my last trip to Paris. She was going to Bosnia, on business. And what about the older gentleman who snored so loudly that I had to kick his sides a few times before I was able to shut my eyes?

Why was I feeling any different this time? Could it be that she was very different from these business people, wearing practically the same types of suits, man or woman? Was it because after almost an hour next to her I knew nothing exciting about her? Or, perhaps it was because she never asked what I do. She avoided the most common question and therefore created the sense or reality for our conversation.

I do not know, but her head was very close to my shoulder and I could smell her hair. It was a good smell, basic but comforting.

I looked at her without moving my head. Her eyes were closed, and she seemed asleep. Then she moved, repositioned herself in the seat as if in response to my inquisitive look. As I tried to look at her again (just as a teenager would do), she opened her eyes and looked back.

This is crazy, I thought. A crazy juvenile game! But, in its innocence, it felt interesting. In some strange way, it seemed like the games we used to play in high school or even prior to those years. Reliving these moments provided a sense of return to moments, places and people.

~ "Where do you live?" she whispered, without opening her eyes.

~ "In Columbia."

~ "You have a great mall! I have been there."

It was so funny that I burst into laughter.

~ "Yes, we have a mall. Some think that it is the center of all culture in Columbia. You know how the burbs are."

There was another moment of silence. And then, in a most natural yet unexpected way she asked:

~ "Do you like my hair?"

—*September 3, 1995*

A Working Woman

~ "Black or white?"
~ "Black" I said.

It was the Costa Coffee Boutique, at Gatwick's South Terminal. I was supposed to have had time to sleep, on this trans-Atlantic flight. "Go away for a week" my wife said, "I will miss you, but it is good for you. Go away from the twins, you will love 'em even more upon return."

But I got the "baby row" on the British Airlines. Four less-than-two-years old, and their child-like mothers. It was noisy, in a happy way. There was life, early. There I was, tired.

Black coffee had full aroma, but my taste buds were sending mixed messages. I guess buds need a good night's rest, too. They were capricious, they were naughty. So much so that my smell receptors soon became erratic. The almond croissant was too dry, the almonds too stale. I had an early morning shadow to shave away.

Yet asleep, I was experimenting with simultaneous efforts of fluid intake and dropping eyelid control. I was about to succeed when I saw her. Or at least saw her back. Or yet saw a back I assumed that of a woman.

And it was. Although could not see her face, her hands were singularity intriguing. It took me a few minutes to make the transition from torpor to pseudo lucidity, to comprehend why her hands were so attractive.

It was not their shape, although they seemed well cared for, the hands of a non-manual worker. Still, they seemed to be engaged in a frantic rhythm of weaving. A virtual Afghan perhaps. Or a pair of socks. Constantly.

Curly auburn hair, late twenties. She looked as if fresh out of bed, after an eventful night. She took her dark wool coat off, showing a dark wool suit. It was of good taste, expensive, abused. A frequent traveler's type of clothing.

She almost rushed to the coffee bar as if caffeine dependency thresholds were becoming symptomatic. I followed her by the corner of my eyes. Strange, still could not see her face. The entire secretiveness had woken me up and now I was genuinely intrigued.

A large crowd of Nordic looking people suddenly filled the area between the bar and my table. I lost her. For a few seconds, I searched for her, but only discovered pale faces, tired of the passage of time, of space, across watery cultural divides. For a second, I was pensive about my own expectations, when I realized that she was back, sitting opposite me, back turned, face unknown.

She was left handed. Nervously, scooped twice out of the brown sugar bowl, and dipped her spoon in the same spot close to the cup's rim. She turned the spoon counter clockwise. I have never known of anyone turning the spoon counter clock wise. I was absolutely taken by the charming, unsuspecting and uncommon movements of this woman.

She drank with the unforgiving passion that only the lack of passion knows. It was a short sip, and another. I fancied about her lips; could not see them, but sure were ample. Perhaps of the early morning dry.

She might have known about the dryness of the almond croissant as she tore apart a fluffy butter croissant. With the nervousness I grew to love, applied a generous layer of butter and one of marmalade. Took a small bite, a quick one. Then, with no warning to my growing curiosity, she
licked each finger on the left hand. No. She sucked on each finger by placing them in her mouth one at a time, up to the knuckles. It was a "geste de tendresse", a geste of alluring impatience.

Behind her, on the illuminated wall of the terminal was a creative Smirnoff Vodka ad. There were three elves fishing in a mountain-framed lake. They had strange facial expressions, their fishing rods were not to scale, and only the "Off" of the label was showing. One had to know about Smirnoff to decipher the message. I was faced with the same dilemma: I saw the back of her head, and like the elves, was fishing for more.

She pulled out a tabloid, and in a hurried but yet non-chalant matter, navigated through the pages. She stopped on one titled "Each day of my life is like hell on earth", and read the story. Why? Was that a state she identified with? Perhaps someone else she knew? I realized that she had two rings on the middle finger of the right hand. The nails were not painted, were short, that of a working person. And although she swirled the coffee left-handed, she flipped through the tabloid pages right handed.

~ "The Roman Catholic Holy Mass will be held in the South Terminal."

59

I was side tracked by the announcement and took my eyes away from her. A "Dorothy Pirkins" shop was on her right far wall of the terminal. A collection of female swim wear were displayed in the window. The contrast between her dark suit and the bra and wraparound - the waist floral beach wear made me fancy: how would she look in them? There was a similarity between her and the mannequins: there were headless, just like her!

~ "Can I share your table?"

I saw the acne-ridden face of a teenager.

~ "Sure."

I shared the faux-marble table top with a young man, still growing. So was I.

I looked at her shoes. femininity is expressed through the shape of shoes. Not their color. Nor the way some women tangle the shoe from their big toe. No. Just the shape. She was wearing squared heel shoes. Black. The type that says nothing about the person. Just like her hair. From the back.

~ "Lover's right to know" was the new tabloid page she read. She was half through the coffee and finished the croissant. She licked each finger, with great charm.

The flight to Amsterdam was announced. I had to leave. Picked my briefcase, threw my coat on my left forearm, and took a step toward her. I had to see her face. But then, stopped. I smiled, almost laughed. Childishly. Like the young man with acne face would. And turned away.

—*March 5, 1996*
Gatwick Airport

Time Is A Very Precious Thing, Love

~ "Oh My Irish Molly O!"

I looked at her, gently sleeping next to me. After a few years, one has to believe in pheromones. That you can smell your mate sleeping content. That you can learn, imperceptibly through the air moved around by the pillow, the comforter, that she is having a good dream. Or just no problems.

It was a night like so, early in March. The El Niño weather pattern had shifted things around: crocuses were out, daffodils about ready to show their colours. We even left the windows open at night. And, we grilled chicken thighs and drank Mexican beer with lime in the froth. On the deck.

Then, went to bed. The wind was from the North, and our dog had settled in the lower part of the bed. A third person, for sure! Almost six years now, since I brought that homely mutt from a Maryland farm. Almost eighty pounds now, and the loveliest pooch any one with four year old twins would want.

~"Oh my Irish...."

I knew she was asleep, for I know when she is. It is that rhythm one leans to detect, to dissociate it from the cadenced breathing of the dog upon the bed, the occasional apnea any of the co-habitants of this bed may experience, and the unpredictable sounds the dogwood tree branches make, outside the open window. And yet, my mind was racing, and I could not take my eyes away from the TV.

Yes, it was good ol' Paddy, the golden tenor of Ireland. I knew him well, for he was part of our friend's life for many years. A friend who died two Christmases ago, on Christmas day. A friend who was Ireland for us, before we met with her in Dublin. Then she became one with the drift of the water falls, she has built in her backyard. "Bigger than a handkerchief, lovely as a button" her backyard was.

We arrived on a sunny day, to Dublin. I had not seen her for more than 5 years, since I left the Persian Gulf. We worked there; we celebrated Christmas there; and it was in that desert that we realized that the green island, no matter how struggling for showing the path to lost angels, was home. For my friend, it was where her childhood had survived; for me it was the birthplace of my friends good humor.

~ "There you are. Not a bit changed. Oh well, a bit perhaps" she said, " and you are just lovely, Janet! What a grand idea you had to pass by. Let's go home and celebrate. Yes love," she turned to me' " you can put your luggage in the booth. If you can open it. I know you liked to tinker with mechanical things..!

My wife was feeling Irish, perhaps for the first time in her life. She never really thought of herself as such; just and American girl born to parents of Irish names, Irish looks, Irish love of life. Hard workers, for sure, but Americans. That morning, she realized that she was Irish. Perhaps there are cultural pheromones one submits to, when the wind if from the rocky shores of the Island. Or it is the winding roads, the sheep, the jolly faces one is offered in welcome. I do not know, but have often felt, that when in Ireland, even an Armenian has tendencies toward feeling Irish. Even if for a short while...

We learned, that very day that forever was a long, long time away, and that when the heart is to sharing, the hand is to giving. We had Gin from Cork, we had lamb from the green side of the mountain, and we talked about what we wanted to have. "I have it now, love" she said" this is my home, seven clouds away from God."

A few years later she called me to say that she had a brain tumor. Two months later her sister wrote to me that "she was lovely, even while dying."

~ "The Fields of Athenry" was the next song. By then, I was wide awake, and so was my wife. She squinted, rearranged her pillow, put her chin upon my shoulder, and said "Do you remember?"

Do I?

~ "I have been thinking about that myself," I said, "but thought you were asleep, so kept quiet."

~ "I was, but could not pass this song. So many years already, goodness!"

Yes, it was many moons ago, when she gave that tape to us.

~ "Paddy Reilly is a good man" she said, "remember Ireland when you listen to him."

So we did, almost a decade later, on a March night, in Maryland. The wind was from the North, and the window was open. I could almost smell the daffodils ready to open their crowns. There was moisture in the air from last night's rain, and it brought me closer to the my thoughts, my remembrances.

62

~ "May God bless her soul" my wife said when the song was over. "Good night love."

And within minutes she was back to where only peaceful souls can go so quickly. And I listened to the rhythmic breathing she acquired as a sign of a restful night. I turned the TV off, put the remote control next to the alarm clock, and turn it on. Then crossed my arms behind my head and looked outside. A clear night, a moonlit night, a night when lonesome souls find their song, and perhaps the waterfall in the backyard, which was bigger than a handkerchief, and lovely as a button.

Then, when all was sleeping around me, slowly got off the bed, walked downstairs, found a bottle of Jameson, a clean glass, and sat in front of the closet where old tapes are often thrown. "Only if.." I thought.

And it was there, the yellow jacketed cassette, "The Fields of Athenry"!! Had a sip, let a shiver run down my spine, and inserted the cassette into the kids' "Little Mermaid" tape player. When I placed the earphones on my head and pushed "Play", I thought I heard my friend say "Think of Ireland when you listen to Paddy."

Well love, that night in March, I thought about Ireland, and in a way that perhaps only two people can understand, I cried in my soul. Not because of what happened to you, but because of what your memory has become.

—*March 14, 1998*

Hay on Dirt, Grows Grass

~ "You are here! It is you!"

Exactly a decade had passed since I left Ann Arbor, Michigan. By no planning on my part, I returned to lecture at a University where fifteen years ago I was a student. It was the anniversary of my exodus toward the real world of America, a land so large that it took me a decade to cris cross. As a researcher, as a curious man.

Goodness, I thought, she has not changed a bit. Perhaps thinner. I thought about the 14 pounds I have accumulated in the past decade. And the gray in my beard.

I landed in Ann Arbor by mistake. In 1982, while working in the Persian Gulf as an epidemiologist, I returned to the American University of Beirut for meetings. Then Beirut got encircled, surrounded. It was July, Ramadan, hot, humid, without water, rats in the street eating garbage, cadavers, other rats. It was shelling of innocent people hidden in innocent basements, it was hot, it was Ramadan, it was civil war.

I was young and immortal. Like most residents of West Beirut, I quickly picked up a hobby I had left behind in 1978 when I went to Qatar: guessing where the rockets, bombs, shells, and anti-aircraft loads will land and explode. We could tell from the whistling sound, the cringing noise, or the level of silence it created if we would be able to meet at Kiriakos's place that night for a few drinks. In one piece that is. Still having the same number of friends.

We were immortal, in 1978. Even when we collected body parts and threw them in the back of a Dodge pickup, we were immortal. And we were numb. It really helped.

In July of 1982, I realized that my immortality was running out of breath. I was getting worried about the mortar shells falling around the Public Health building on campus. I even got afraid when a group of armed thugs asked me if I could get syringes for them from the veterinarian floor, at the basement of the building. I was young, yet the proud carrier of many thoughts about the essentials of living. Today, these events are still getting their share of maturation in my remembrance. I know much happened during these days, but will wait till when I know what they meant. For now, it is important to note that

64

I did not even have time to say good bye to my family when I left Beirut. Couldn't even call them that I was leaving in a yellow, 8 cylinder Dodge Dart '74. No, we had to leave that very morning, five of us, myself being the only non-American. Three women, two men. I asked a friend to let my parents know that I had left for Damascus, Syria. I had a student visa, obtained by luck from the last employees of the American Embassy still in the building that was later on destroyed by a booby trapped truck. I remember shells falling in the distance, and there were hundreds of us waiting in line at 5 am, like poorly planted tulips around a garage wall. We would not give our space to anyone, unless the shells explode so close that we see shrapnel denting the concrete walls or our ear drums ringing like a hand hammered bronze church bell in Jourat Ballout, in the Lebanese mountains. And even then, the tinnitus of approaching disaster may have paled compared to the prospect of getting a visa. To America, by George, to America!

~ "If you do not smoke, I will give you 25 additional pounds bakhshish (tip)."

The poor taxi driver was nervous as chipmunks are when they see our neighbor's cats. And the public health professor in the yellow Dodge Dart was ignoring the dangers we were about to face driving through the Lebanese mountain back roads to Syria. "Smoking is bad both for you and us" he continued, "have you not heard of second hand smoking?"

Although the driver was tempted to eject the professor and his daughter from the car, he swallowed hard through his drying throat and continued. I remember him stopping a couple of times "to check the tires." When he opened the hood, we thought the car was on fire, only to realize that he was chain smoking as fast as he could..

The trip to the Syro-Lebanese boarder, the usual impossible problems that can only be cured with money rolled as if cigarettes; with cartons of Marlboro (the driver had a few in the trunk, knowing the unwritten protocol); or loafs of freshly baked Lebanese pita breads that emerged from the same famous trunk. I will never forget the expression of content on the face of our driver when he was offered hot red tea, filled with sugar, and lit his Marlboro. He looked at the professor and exhaled the most copious amount of smoke from his nostrils. Kind of a challenge from an urban dragon of war.

Then to Frankfurt, then to Detroit.

~ "Welcome to America" an African American customs officer said, "Ann Arbor is a neat town. You'll like it."

I wanted to sleep. I was overwhelmed with the amount of light, everywhere. With new smells, with new air. After Beirut-with-no-electricity-no-water, the opulence of everything, all the time was overwhelming. Decadent. I wanted to cry. Say that for running water mothers were waiting in line, in July, in Beirut, with a newborn in their arms. For hours. And here, in the men's room of the Detroit airport, people were leaving the water run non-stop from the faucet while they checked their teeth in the mirror! I wanted to sleep, but still had to get to Ann Arbor.

~ "Your motel!" she said jumping out of the truck. How many bags?" I signaled one with my index finger. "Al the way to the U.S. with only one bag? My- my, you should have a lot in your head!"

I did. But first, I needed a good night's rest.

The receptionist was a middle aged woman. "How many nights?" She asked.

~ "Just one. Tomorrow I am going to the University."

She smiled, and extended her left arm for a "welcome" shake. I realized that her right arm was missing.

When I went to bed that night, I was wondering where were all these tall, blond, athletic women we thought America was made of ?....

I woke up, in a motel on Washtenaw Road, on September 3, 1983. Looked out of the window, and nothing was moving. There were no cars, no traffic, no people dressed as the gangs in West Side Story, no people jogging. I remember how crisp everything looked, so colorful is Ann Arbor in early Fall! And the new smells, in the motel, in the air. I was almost light-headed.

I had more for breakfast that morning then I have had for a week in Beirut, a few days back. The coffee was terrible (after 15 years, still is!), but the rest was unbelievably wholesome. Having traveled extensively, many of the aspects were familiar, but still distinctive. Perhaps I had lost familiarity with the basics of live between Qatar and Beirut. Perhaps these were not the basics of life. Rather the extras, the plenty I was not used to.

My one-arm-lady was gone. I was ready to discover the University. And an hour of walk later, I was on South Campus, in the midst of thousand of young people, healthy looking people, people with leather-bottom backpacks. I was a student again!

~ "How do you like the music?" a heavy set, freckled face, middle aged woman asked me.

~ "Hurts my tympans" I replied borrowing from my then second language, French.

For the rest of that first acquaintance party for doctoral students, all my colleagues made fun of me and the "tampons" in my ears. And, it was just the beginning of such inter-linguistic innuendoes. Over the years, I have told people that I had taken a "douche"; that my "feet fingers" were cold; or that it was at that party that I met my friend, and soon after her husband. And, over the years we remained in touch, curious about many things.

Ten years later, I hugged my professors good night, at the Gandy Dancer. One of them is the man who gave our '74 Dodge taxi driver a hard time about smoking, fifteen years ago. He still looks grand: just a bit more gray. I looked at him drive away, on this crisp October night, in his Mercury.

Back to my room at the Weber's Inn, an Ann Arbor historic site. Called home, inquired about the kids, the day, the mail. Then, realized that it was only 10 o'clock, and I was wide awake. In some ways, I was excited about the Obstetrics Grand Rounds I was doing next morning. I do not get the butterflies, the ants, or the creeps before presentations any more. Unfortunately, things have a way of getting routinized, predictable. But that night I did. I think it was being back in town, dinner with those who controlled my student life for a few years, the Weber's Inn where my wife and I used to go as students, for a drink. Perhaps it was that thought that got me out of my room, and to the Inn's bar.

At first sight, the environment seemed very familiar. Probably nothing had changed in the entrance to the bar. Same dark shellacked wood panels, dim lights, Mexican "Tiffany" colored-glass lamps, the smell of cigarette smoke. Walked to the bar, took the stool next to the large column.

A few older people were having dinner. The entire atmosphere was one of order, cleanliness. About forty feet away was the stage, inundated by red and soft amber lights. A band was performing. Three women, one man. All very young, probably Ann Arbor students.

"You save the last for me...." She was singing. I looked. Yellow short skirt, black, silky panty hoses, and black turtle neck. She was wearing a square-toe shoe, Nordstrom type. Long hair, could not distinguish her facial features. Too dark, too far, not wearing my

67

glasses. But her voice was distinctly average. Actually, she was whispering, rather than singing. A suave, alluring atmosphere, where romantic, now classic songs were offered by four students whose collective age-years would not add to a century.

~ "Hi there. What can I get you?"

Early twenties, flat chested, anybody's daughter. A peach bandana tied around her waist. Black pants, black turtle neck.

~ "Wine, of the red conviction."

~ "Just the stuff for you!" She said, while checking if the glass was spotless. In fact, it was dark enough that I may not have noticed even the smear of lipstick on the edge. "Cabernet or Merlot?"

~ "Surprise me" I said.

~ "My love..my darling..Your touch.." Now it was the boy/man singing while caressing the metal strings on his probably rented guitar. His voice was metallic, probably still in metamorphosis. The woman on the keyboard was moving in a non-chalant way, almost as if in a fake trans. Overall, I could not detect any musical mishaps.

A couple each wearing MICHIGAN sweatshirts left their table and started a dance. A slow dance, looking deep into each other's eyes. Perhaps souls. Did I do the same, I wondered, fifteen years ago? I remember dancing on that same floor. I do not think there was a band. There were more people smoking, that I remember.

~ "There, enjoy!" she said placing the glass of wine on a Weber's Inn napkin. "Good food since 1937" it read. I pulled the napkin from under the glass, took out my pen, and started taking note. I always do. Taking note helps me note the details that go unnoticed. Like the logo on the jacket of the guy sitting next to me at the bar. "Ever Clean. Inc. Snow removal." Or the DUKE on the cap of the student sitting next to the snow removal guy. Or that our barmaid had a pointed nose, delicate mouth, hazel eyes, and a garden-variety auburn hair. That she bit her finger nails.

"You are my herooo.." was now the woman at the keyboard singing. An attractive voice, I thought. The best yet. And I smiled to the guy next to me. He was nursing a sweating mug of beer and had just lit a cigarette.

~ "Are you a writer?" he asked seeing that I was taking note on the napkin.

~ "No, I said, just trying to capture a few thoughts."

~ "Yeah."

He turned his head away, toward the waitress, and seemed to be looking at her for a long time.

~ "I have the same thoughts all the time" he finally whispered, "the same ones. Especially since I got divorced. No need for me to write them down. The same thoughts." And he smiled to the barmaid.

She smiled back. It seemed to me that she had heard him whisper these words before.

~ "What do you do when it does not snow?" I tried to sound curious.

~ "Excavation. This is good time. Here in Michigan. Much building. Heard about the casino stuff in Detroit?

~ "Yeah, I did. I am not sure that will help turn things around, though."

~ "Cannot hurt."

~ "Unforgettable..." Was now whispering the woman with no voice. But, perhaps it was the wine, or the long day, or the looks the excavator was sharing with the twenty-some barmaid, that I found the whispering attractive. Very much so. I stopped writing, looking around. Took another sip, shut my eyes, and remembered the old 78 rpm turn disk table and plates my father had, in Beirut. We had one of Nat's albums. I think it had the hits "Too young" , "Lost April", and "Hajji Baba" on it. The main song was "Unforgettable." My father used to play that disk, often. We did not know English. He knew very little, himself. But it sounded generic, basically omni-cultural. It was about the stuff we all knew, may that be expressed in English, Arabic, French or Armenian. Years later, I understood the words, but realized that I knew the theme of these songs.

~ "Unforgettable, that's what yooooo are.." was now whispering our barmaid while placing a coffee cup under the cappuccino machine. And she did that with the slight undulation of her hips. Of the shoulders. Each in a different direction, at a different tempo. The excavator took another sip on his beer, and I took a few additional notes.

It was at this point that the barmaid gave me a piece of paper.

~ "Wannah use this?'

~ "No" I said "this is more à propos."

~ "Are you a writer?"

~ "No, a teacher."

~ "Cool!" She said and went back to the cappuccino machine.

After filling the other orders for drinks, she came back to me.

~ "What do you teach?"

~ "Public health."

~ "Cool!" she said and left again. She never returned to the same conversation. I realized that I was the odd man out in this crowd. After all, what nerd talks about public health with a twenty some woman, in a dark bar! Perhaps I should have said a poet; or an excavator!!

At that point, the DUKE-guy left.

~ "Study hard" the barmaid yelled after him, "and drive carefully." And then turned to the snow plowing professional "he had two beers tonight. He better be careful. I'll see him in class tomorrow."

~ "Love is made for you and me" was now the song, and I was finishing my second glass of wine. It was close to the time when pumpkins turn into humans, students go home, and I slowly walk to my room.

There was frost on the cars! The air was so crisp, that I decided to walk around the block, first.

And, I continued to think about the times when my wife and I lived a couple of miles from here; when I used to translate from French; when my friend was kind enough to give me her typewriter for my papers.

I realized that I have not stopped typing since...

—*October, 15, 1997*

A Candid Approach To Destiny

I don't remember the first time when I looked at myself as an ant, one among many. Perhaps it was during a camping trip when I was twelve. I came across an ant colony, a very large one. There were thousands of ants, all looking alike. I sat down and for what I recall as hours, observed the ants.

They looked alike, though I knew they were different. Its just that I didn't know how to distinguish. Perhaps that was because I was looking from a distance, looking at the larger picture, where the individual was not important for the character of the panorama. I looked at them work, carry gains, carry dropping, carry twigs. I was very young and unaware of the stories millions before me had recanted about their observations and inspirations from ants at work.

Looking back, I think I have always believed in destiny- in an almost scientific way. Almost factually. Evidence-based. I always thought that it is the group that counts. That in the larger picture of passage —through time and existence, what happened to the individual didn't matter. To matter, it needed a threshold. A critical mass. Either of joy or misery. But a threshold. It needed a genocide to change history, not the death of a person.

And to test that idea, I killed an ant. I left the dead ant where it died. It is often better that way. Even for people. Perhaps the passage gets easier. Perhaps not. I kept looking at the ants. Thousands of them. Couldn't notice any change in their behaviors. There were long lines of ants where each ant seemed to patiently pace the speed of its legs. There were those going into the hole, always from one side of the opening. Others coming out, from the other side. Sort of a gentleman's understanding of how traffic works on a two-way street. Perhaps they cursed, called each other "roach!" Perhaps all this was anthropomorphic. There were no physical assaults on each other during that traffic time. That I could see.

So, why did the one ant die? For no real reason, other than that all of them will die, at some time. That one's timing was unique. Perhaps every ant's timing is unique. Perhaps time doesn't matter. What did that one ant do to the colony, the larger population of time-bound ants? Seemingly nothing. Maybe it was a lonely ant. Perhaps it was the unfriendly type. Or perhaps, friends and family didn't hear

the news to run and see him. Perhaps ants do not have friends. Who
knows? The important thing was that a twelve year old boy, in the
mystical mountains of Lebanon, in a village called Beit-Mery, decided
that day to believe that populations change destiny. He also believed
that the destiny of individuals couldn't be changed- just that of groups,
by having the people of similar destiny come together at the appropriate
time. By chance.

Since that day, almost three decades have passed. I passed
through one civil war. Came out of it. Every time a Howitzer shell
exploded a few yards away, I thought about the city, the people. Not
myself. It was not important for that war to continue or end. I counted
the bullet holes in the concrete of the buildings- as if I were counting
snapdragon blossoms. It was to pass time, not to change it.

I have since changed countries, more than once. Even changed
nationality. I waited in line for filling out forms, for interviews, for
acceptances, for rejections. In each waiting time, I looked at the people
around me and thought about the ants. I also played a funny game, the
one I learned to play during the civil war. I called it "reaching the
threshold for dissociation." Here is how it works:

When people get too antsy around me, I place myself in a rocket
and shoot it in the air. High. Way up. As I get higher, people
disappear. What remains is the larger picture. And I look down at it,
and I see it change. As destined. Irrespective of what people did. I
enjoy the serenity of the moment. And then, come back down. Pack
my sputnik somewhere away from people, and mix with them again
—without having left them in the first place. But now much more
accepting. Much more clairvoyant.

The threshold for dissociation varies across people. I also think
that it changes in amplitude with time. In a way the reverse of habitual
dependency, such as on stimulants. Both internal and self administered.
I think the threshold for dissociation increases in amplitude with its
usage. We need it less frequently. We learn to live with reality. With
people. With ourselves. We do so because we increasingly believe in
destiny. That the group will go where it is supposed to go. Eventually.
Perhaps will take a few detours. Will be delayed. But it will get there.

Destiny has different names. Sometimes it is a rain-dance, other
times it is a nuptial embrace. Destiny is often rejected, only to be
discovered later- when the joints ache in the morning. When the joints
ache in prediction of the coming rain. Destiny is for the lived, for the
living. It is to age what age is to time. It is to the nest what the nest is

to the tree. Destiny is also a time for reflection. Ultimately, for the wise and the wisening, destiny is truth, in its capricious splendor. In its timing.

Western medicine is just discovering the role of destiny in health. Genetics and microbiological sciences are to be credited for such a cultural transformation of medicine. We now teach about oncogenes, hereditary pre-disposers to pathological manifestations as well as behavioral profiles. In response to these pre-programmed potentials for dis-ease, people are taking action. Sometimes haphazardly. There are prophylactic mastectomies, hysterectomies, soon perhaps prostatectomies. There is a steep rise in people's recourse to alternative medicine. Western medicine is discovering destiny. Medical students are now taught how to deal with probabilities. They learn about statistics, odds ratios, chance. They map genes, genome, think about the inherited code. The one that makes you become yourself. The one that over times makes you become your parents. And eventually, makes you reflect the group. The colony. Like the ants on that mountain in Lebanon.

But with the discovery of destiny, a number of old issues are resurfacing. Among these is the concept of immortality. There may be a departure from the sole concept of individual immortality. Based on some behavior prior to mortality. While the pre-programmed code was getting organized. Within the body's cells. Through inheritance. The immortality of a group, of a group's ideal, is perhaps becoming of interest. The colony vis à vis the ant. An old concept. Sounds brand new though.

Destiny's counterpart is immortality, not representing the absence of death, but the presence of the dead within the living. In a vivid way, in ways subtle and unmarked. Through sex. Sexuality is the transformer of destiny and assurer of immortality. Did that ant have sex? Did it share its genetics with another ant? Other ants? Will he live in shape, mind and soul in another ant, or an interminable number of ants? Forever? Or, did that ant go with his genes unshared? Perhaps he just worked all his life. No sex. And then, my index finger pushed him down. To mortality. Through destiny.

No matter, though, the other ants will mix their genes, their pains and vitality into the pool of ant chromosomes. In a down-to-earth way. Will have sex while working, on the job, in front of family and friends.

Will have sex alone, in a soft hole in the ground, surrounded by grain, twigs, and
bird droppings. The perfect romance for ants. And they will work for the colony, the larger picture. And that is what remains, what prospers. Through rainy season and drought. Through robins, ant eaters, lizards and frogs.

I eventually became a public health worker. An immigrant ant, who by destiny was isolated from the colony to work in other colonies of immigrant ants. For these ants. I became an epidemiologist. I placed the group at the forefront. I measured the group's characteristics. Their diseases. Their mortality. Their birth patterns. As a colony. Sometimes, I thought about the gene pool, about my gonads, about others' gonads. I leaned to observe and be patient. Work. It is always good for the pace of destiny. I knew love, and learned to be loved. By ants from different colonies. And then left.

Immortality is a process, the boundaries of which are uniform. I have thought about immortality of groups, through their diseases and death. Rarely of individuals. Except for poets. Except for poets who shared their genetic code as a rhyme. That I recite. That others do. Over the years. Because of the immortality of a rhyme. Because the poets write of destiny. Unavoidably. Because their sexuality is about destiny. Because poets have sex with destiny. They make love to it. They make peace with it.

I sometimes look up to see when an index finger will push me down. To the colony's ground. An immigrant Armenian epidemiologist. His destiny written on his forehead.

—*May 1996*

74

Okole Maluna
(And a few poems. . . .)

Circadian Prophecy

To remain coupled
To change
As if under the signs
Of passing clouds
The granite mountain
Had embraced its dark shadow
Of shame
As a cover for its sons
In a grave cadence
For cavalcade unswerving passages
Inward
When freedom
Was the prophet
At a crossed path
On the shores
Of wavering lust
For lips of the embrace still bruised
And shoulders of the snivel fretted
Eternity was a plate
In its circle entrenched
Where grief tore its own
Hair in disdain
And where the sound of a newborn man
Found the tremor
Of aging hips
Yet untouched
By the passage of men
By the rain upon fields fecund
Of seeds and vast spaces
For March hail had broken the burgeon
Off ancestral twigs

—February 7, 1997

Koumandaria

In memory of the Wine Festival of 1979 in Limassol, Cyprus

The boat took us to Limassol
Where Turkish waves die on Greek sand
Homeless, as driftwood do when they can only drift.
And when I drank the Koumandaria wine
I knew that of the old vines the soul I had drank.

Your neck of beads adorned, your breast warm and free
In your sandals, your youth, in your kalithea
I drowned the moment, as if an evening bath
Of the last ray over roofs of red clay,
Of an aging Lebanese hamlet.

In barrels of oak, in vessels of time
I transformed your face into a name, and a sound.
Tall glasses piled high upon my head
I danced, the singles' dance of Crete
Where every yassou also means pethimou.

I left you where I found you, bouboulina,
Holding the silver sipper of its own chain bound
To a cask, a barrel, or to time itself
Time we had to know that when wine is plenty

Promises dance the dance of forgiveness
In Limassol

—December 28, 1997

Quand tu Songe

When you sleep do you tremble, dear
As the mango trees in nights of spice and powder did
When the dust was of angels, when you burned your fingers
Trying to point to yourself through the broken glass of youth

When you sleep do you surrender, dear
As the gypsy child did to her father that night
Upon the combed sand of a beach too old
Upon the seat, upon the rags which once covered your chest

When you sleep, I tremble dear
'For of that sand my dreams are often filled
For of the sounds I never recall my soul still vibrates
As a string you pulled with the finger you often burned

When I sleep, dear, I cannot sleep
My bed is never mine, and my pillow has your face
Still engrooved upon as if the combed sandy beach
Where the gypsy girl surrendered, a warm morning in March

The world over I crossed
To Carry you in me

—March 27, 1998
Air India Flight 101
Mumbai to London

Land Marks

The stones were held by time
Through which rays abundantly reflected
Upon moments when it was easy
To hold time responsible for the shadow
The bridge extended peacefully
The bridge made of stones held together by moss
Through which evening blooming Jasmin in harmony and Dance
In lines that enwrap upon themselves
To shape the moment in scent as we once did
Upon the pond next to the bridge
A summer day when the golden evening rays
Sparkled within your tender sweating breasts
And shivered under my casual touch

There were wild apple trees where I left my bike
Where I lost my time I had kept for myself
I lost it through you, in you, for you
The precious bundle of time I kept together in me
For when I would not have enough time to keep
As the stones did for the bridge now covered with moss
Covered in dreams of sleeps past
When on steamy August nights girls wore cotton dresses
And tickled the pond with their toes painted in pastel
Colours
As their lips became after the kiss and gentle bite
Adorned of the evening blooming Jasmin and the mist upon the pond
Next to the wild apple trees
Where I left my bike lying on its side

While you stole my time
Under the bridge held together
By the courtesy of time
And moss

—May 27, 1998
Amtrak #145
Trenton NJ to BWI

79

Aegyptium

A veil of scent swaddled in your breasts
As I covered your hair with the nuptial cloud
Of knowing you, simple maudlin of the sea
Where every port ached into a bloom of desire to be at
Your side and decide
To build that cedarwood ship and hear the caterwaul of the sea froth
Upon the flanks of rehearsing emotions I have holding
Your hips, into a balance.

I read love backwards while I covered your acorn
With lavender, neroli, and almond-oil
In windblown motions as the flux of unda upon the golden sand have
known
To calm the daimon in men still of hips adorned, still of
Tender bellies ashamed.
And, as you emerged of the nuptial bath in peace,
Of clay and henna your torrential hair I toned, in forgiveness.

In your name I called the green wines of peace "Spasms Of
Sandalwood Fire"
For my soul you used as burner of the scent
Of the sea, of the chest where hungry mouths have
Searched

The comfort of the known as sons of the wind, as dunce,
As lonely man who found you almond-oiled and sweet
Petals ringed,
In every port.

—April 6, 1997

Cor homini

No sea will ever calm
Before a storm engulfs
The sand
Where your tremor
I found
And froth in your waves

No mountain ever forms
Without the clash of rocks
Where granite gods
Drink from the chalice of men
And cry tears so old
That old lakes get deep

No sky ever gets dark
Without the clouds of time
That erase the torment
And pass
As the passage of fear
On your face
Forms age and rime

No child ever forgets
The shiver of death
On his mother's lips
When a stranger shines
A homemade blade
On her lonely face

No leave will ever fall
In the summer of life
And you will have to
Wonder and pounce
For I am to time
What cadence and rime
Are to the whirling
Dance of fall

—*October 21, 1995*

Jbeil in June

In the distance, a churchyard captures the shades of dark
As I hold you, without the tremor that once remembered
Our Embrace
In anticipation of the touch, a journey to the known
We tried to forget, as in spring dogwood trees do,
Of the frigid drain of snow, through their roots.

The songs I wrote were about a wounded swallow,
Remember?
Or of the eve where a nest was woven, twig upon twig,
Weed by weed,
To harbor the loneliness I brought to you, in fulfillment,
In fear
That red moons bring back faces we forgot to remember.

The churchyard still holds, dear, the serenade of the day
When our touch reached the wounded swallow
When our chest harbored a damaged nest, and mended,
Twig by twig, weed upon weed, tear by tear
The time to love every departure, too soon!
From the churchyard
Where the shades of dark carried the image of
Tomorrow's,
The scent of you on the pillow, where I spoke of love to
You

And said goodbye,
For I did not belong
To the time you had for the shades of dark
And red moons

—April 24, 1997

83

In The New England Woods

Friend, pass by the trail
When the sun is low
And in its scarlet breath
Panting.
Under the elm tree
We left a branch
Undisturbed,
To become one
With itself.
Drink from the spring
That one sunny day will
Break its own water
And become water again.
Smell the autumn scents
On the acorn tree, hanging
As if Spanish moss of May
Or your hair on my chest.
Brave the new paths we found
But never had time to step,
For our moment was full
Of memories to come.
And when the sun is low
In its quotidian tour,
Search the clouds for rain
Or the returning dove.
That is the moment we never had.
It is not late, dear friend,
To have it all alone.

—February 7, 1994

It Is Not The Same Anymore

Sleep on my side
New companion and friend.
You died, lived again,
In a new shape and happy eyes.

I often pray that you
May be back,
Get your wet nose closer
For we spend a decade of love.
Bend your arm under your chin
And let me guess about your dream.

Place your caring head
On my lap and shoulders.
I saw your brown eyes open
To the joy of a day of play.

I wish we could grow older, old companion
But remain close and tender.
Let youth run itself tired
While we both sit by the fire.

And when it is time to sleep
Of that earthly, deep sleep
That you will let me be there, again.
You are my share
You are my love, dear parting friend.

You have no tomb where I can cry,
You have no sky where I can fly,
But when I find a grayish hair
On my pillow, in my car, or cotton shirts,

I still cry. You were so dear,
My Chalo dog!

—February 7, 1994

85

Anthropocentric is the Red Sea
To: Avédis and Dorothy
In memory of a past we separately share

From Beit Fajjar
To Abu Dis
The barren hills roll
In peace
Over a rocky sea
Waved by anemone
And
White umbellifers

Time has no pride
To stop for respite
On the limestone side
Of history
Terraced
By the biblical passage
Of men planting vines
And gray-green
Olive trees
In rows
To oppose
The mosaic of thoughts
That carried
Or buried
The olive branch

Like the figwort
Blooming in its dust
Like the purple crucifers
Joining roots and of sun
Imbibed
In Salam
In Shalom
And through untold romance
The bedouin passed
Over this land of hope

And in his path
Remained
Alone

Like the Ophrys orchid
Daughter of the warmest sun
On this Mediterranean shore
Still hides
Beneath rocks
In its splendor
Wild

I played in those fields
Of Phoenicians and Judea
In that red sea of tulips
Away from the mother sea
I reached the desert
Parted by men
And through men
United

Where Adonis broke his
Arrow
I left my youth to dream
Somewhere between white stones
And cattail bushes
In hope to find those times
Again

As if night blooming
Jasmine
Filling the space
Of humid August nights

But, time rode a
Passing cloud
And spring swallows
Cut the thick air
In dance
I lost my youth

In vain
Somewhere
Between the sea of tulips
And the sea port
Of pain

—June 4, 1994

Of Stony Places and Mortal Souls

As you sleep
Pearled, fretful and
Alone
Let no song chant
The ode of passage
To your soul
Possessed by its
Evanescence.

You know it will come
The day dark, humid and
Long
When departure in itself
Gets ready
While presence in time
Becomes curtsy
To memory.
When your inner
Timepiece
Stops

Do not remember,
For memories are like cyclamen
In the shade of a rock.
When disturbed,
They shiver, hugging
The midday
Sun.
Do not look into
Springs fluid around
Mossy pebbles.
They once were
Boulders in search
Of water.
And, while you drink, the torment
Renews its tranquil
Roll

And time covers the pebble
Paths
Of interrupted passages.
Do not, friend, move the old air
Yet trapped
Deep in your lungs.
Keep a breath from stony places
So tenderly, as if surprised
That the earth inhales
Its own fragrance
Washed by morning dew
From tulips, weeds, and abandoned
Day Lilly.

Listen to the fall
Of your inner misty garden
You built of gravel
And despair,
Where sweet flag and anacharis
Peeked their pistils
To populate your thoughts.

Just
Listen to the waterfall
Listen to the fall

When you sleep
Pearled, fretful and
Alone

—*June 19, 1994*

The Hand You Were Dealt

Touch your hips
And wake up slow
With your toes pull down
The cover till your breasts
And then rest
Some more
Call my name
When the brook trout
Spat a fly of horsetail hair
And arched its back in vain
Like we did
Dance the wet dance
When the sky is fluffy
Of early spring clouds
When rivers pace and race
In memory of rain
And pink cyclamin bulbs
Think of stem, leaves and buds.
Between two ash trees
Our hammock
Still swings
Hug a man
When you should not.
When morning dew shines
The wild mushroom caps and covers
Fallen bark and April moss.
Open yourself and with warm lips
Accept, offer and be
Perhaps the hoodoo friend
Of destination unknown
And of destiny annoyed
Bury your nose in my neck
Like you would smell a baby
Upon hugging, after a nap.
And realize how age has us
In wrinkles, in pain, in morning breath
And in vain

For the rivers have carried
Rainwater
Cyclamin bulbs have since opened
Their pink flowers
And wild mushroom
Did collapse under heavy
Morning dew.
But, still touch your hips
And wake up slow
Hold my toes in your toes
And in somnolence smile.
Alas, I am your destiny

—March 29, 1994
Philadelphia Train Station

Only a Visit

Don't steal my time
I have yet to run
In brooks engorged of rain
Cast to the brown trout
And bring my day home

Don't help me remember
How I spent my youth
I have yet to inhale
The sweet dogwood bloom
In morning dew embalmed

Don't lead me where you are
The winds never bring back
Clouds of past skies
And Spanish moss waves
Only to ocean breath

Don't, in your youth assume
That the passage will last
For it is said to hide
Beneath the moments of time
As does ivy to pine

I want to stay. But see,
It is my time to be
Of new adventures shy
Of pleasant sounds distant
As your passage and mine
A summer night will part
Apart, and know.

So, don't.
Let me be
Of that very passion
Free

—April 7, 1994

Summer in the South

Where time takes time
To shake the blossom
Magnolia, lilac or roses
From their pistil to the trout pond

Where time stands still
Like a novice on virgin's breast
Cold like the carpenter's glue
On yet of the cut dusty cherry wood

Where time rings a bell
For passages to remember well
That when plump lips are kissed too long
Like roses in May, in pride they glow

Where time to its funeral goes
After passages, novice love, and spring rays
On its fresh sandy mound
Eternity drops tears for the good old
Passed times

—May 5, 1995

Kalskoya

Sea
River
Land
The dying mountains of Kamchatka wash the aching soul
Of a brown bear
On the shore of Kalskoya
Where the aging salmon fly
One more time in Kamtchatka

At the center of the lake
He deposited his heart
As a miracle finds believing eyes among men
Who touch the tender belly of an unknown woman
Upon the shores of a lake
Where the sun sets
In the eyes of a dying bear
Under the mountains of Kamtchatka

—July 13, 1998

The Indian Rope at the Beguinage

I will climb
To disappear
In your wink
Shy and unwanted
As the channel is wet
Of the river and mist
Upon stony walls
Which kept us alone

Oh, dear child I want
Of your youth make a sail
And engage warm August nights
Into a swirl
As silent as the channel is of mossy cobbles
In winter
When short women in poverty
In chastity
And in acceptance
Wrap themselves in rays
Of a frigid sunset
Shielded by the vitrailles
Of the cold room
Still resonating the cracking
Spiral wooden stairs make
Under aging toes and bony knees

I have made a decision, dear,
To leave you and your youth
Near the old streets of Leuven
And find my own channel back
Where white stones flower cyclamen
While the river runs North

Where love is
And where my kids
Shall never again
Grow alone

—October 20, 1998
British Airways Flight #223
London to Washington

Rio Paraguay

In the white of his smile poor men's sun was setting
When I held him tight for I was holding myself
Years later

He put his fingers in my mouth and I kissed them, long,
I knew he would smile
I knew he would cry
The child of the present
The child of a moment, in a dusty house, next to the brown river
Where on a raft he passed alone
Got a first bath in the river
While without fanfare
His mom threw the afterbirth toward Fermosa
On the other side of the brown river

It is sunset now and on my lips
His fingers quiver just as into his eyes my reflection returns
As I held him tight
For I was holding myself
For once I held my son
For once I held my love
Without fanfare
As he might had a bath

On the brown river which divides
The common time
Into personal moments

—October 21, 1998
Fermosa
Argentine/Paraguay Border town

Blue Sandpaintings

Tonight, I feel mellow and eager I am for your hips
As melting snow is to the mossy rock from which it drips
Upon still frozen snow, on sunny days of early spring
While the path to the stream crackles under my amorous
Steps
Toward you

The bath is ready and of enoli incensed, warm and
Inviting
As the words I hope to share as your cadenced breath will Bring
To my lips of past shivers still numb, as frozen trees often
Are
When the North wind brings a scent, oh of past springs
Still alive
Toward you

The chalice is full, the chalice you once made of clay
Holding in your palm the moist shape of a thought you
May
Again have tonight, as the bath will immerse itself in you, Steaming!
As Malbec grapes trap lost rays on the flat hills of Rioja
Away from you

I feel mellow, yet I am not who I once was, eager and
Prime
In hopes of you. See, I have time to let you steal my
Precious time
As in the warmth of life's North winds the chalice has

Dried to a core
In my palm, which toward you I have extend, without
Hurry, in luxury
Of having you

—January 26, 1999

Flash Flood

To the core
Of an age old sore
I descend when a name
Shows my soul the way

Strange, I found my self
Held by the candle in my hand
As its flame flickering
As the wax washes my skin of your touch

I never found your name where I left it
As an echo in the core of a granite wall
Where no other name was etched
Just a halt, an open space where time got whirled

And polished its own edges into boulders of vast sounds
Upon themselves placed by the passage of a familiar
Name
Of you, my introspection and myself, one as lilac petals
Are
When in blossom and when they shiver alone bathing in
The sun

And the core of that still aching old sore I still visit
While my pain has lessened and of the travel
I now am weary. Strange, see, along the walls
Of still a very somber thought of you I search

For the touch we had touched but discovered
Only when of oceans distant the songe of you became
As the shady moss harbors dormant cyclamen
Yet the oak tree falls alone of the North wind

Yet the pond shivers the death of an image
You upon its wrinkles reflected in thought
It was August and in your eyes
Summer was ample as your hips once were

Satin and nue
When to the core
Of a, alas! new sore
I found a name

And it was not yours!

—*October 10, 1998*

Autumn Sonata

I hope to die as a poet
Who found the sound a nipple makes
Upon the lips of aging men
As water finds the clouds to rain
Upon clouds
Upon a time bound in its shape
On the wall
In the hall
Of a nursing home
In search of Wagner
In search of peace

I could die as pigeons die
Crashed upon the citadel of Notre Dame
Aya Sophia or Stefansdom
On Sunny days
Or when
Sailors sell their old pipes
In Amsterdam
To buy cheap rhum
Or a long kiss
From dark lips
Kissed by many

I want to die
As if my life got rid of me
Of my songs
Of my dance in arms I knew
On chests I found under wool blouses
Warm on misty days
In lands new
In lands apart
In moments that became time
Time to stay
Time to stray
Till I had to leave
Till I had to forgive

I know I will die like we all do
Un-accepting, reluctant, afraid, and cursing
For I will know
That someone else will find the words
To my poem
Sailors will kiss the lips
Of Augusta, Morella or Lila
Without selling their hopes
Or their accordion
To men of many women
To women who pay the rent
Of younger men
And then, I will leave
For I will have
Nothing to take

—October 3, 1997
Austrian Airlines #501
Vienna to New York

Chinese New Year

The time I kept for you
Has filled the space of us
As summer showers do
When silk lines reflect the moment
Introspective and disparate
As the time we let under the peach tree
When upon your freckled chest
I placed a sort of a kiss

You opened to me
As the silk lines once did
To the time it caught as the passing thought
Of you got entangled in itself
Searching for the tremor my lips
Felt upon your chest
When the evening sun warmed
The nectar of summer peaches
As they prepare to bath in the moon

The time I kept for you has lost the space
As we separately passed by
The serpentine paths where memories
Of us dusted
The moment of its own burden

Where did our moment go, love?
See the mid-summer sun has burned
The silk lines where your name was caught
As if the memory of you
I keep upon my lips
As a sort of a kiss

—September 14, 1998
Singapore

104

Eleventh Year

In the tumult of your comber
I fell, and lost the sphere
Of no center
Of no rhythm
Monozygotic, as vagabonds are
Before metamorphosis
Into troubadours
In the parking lot of a gothic cathedral
Suckling the brown bag
Which holds their murmur

I would love you as agape,
As Iblyss,
Elemental woman born of a lotus leaf
Or from a thought of you I had
When the shadows discovered
The shades of my youth
And the raven,
Perched upon the spleen
Of the moment eternal

In you I will become reborn of my own entrails
As men do when the call
Covers the sounds of orange blossoms
Blossoming
In secret,
And hold the morning dew
Where lost stars reflect
Upon the moment
They never had
To shine

And in you, agape,
I will find the space
Where no fear, no remorse, and
No trial
Project their tentacles,

Amoebic,

Around the pulse
Of which you are
The name
And the tremor
And the death

—*July 18, 1997*

Furta Sacra
(Holy Theft)

Let's hold hands, hold our deep lifelines
As troubadours held the drawn catgut strings
Of round belled lutes
To reach their souls' counterpart
Intrepid, anti-agape
In affirmation of the image
Of forty pagan philosophers
I drowned in your eyes

Let's wet our shirts from the rhythm of us
And roll the sleeves
As a trembling lip
Placed upon the burning foreheads
Of freckled-breast virgins
Abandoned in the suburbs of another's
Eden

Let's listen to the frown Nina makes
Upon covers of smoky velvet
When of the lonely journey sailors return
Or when star-eyed, pigeon-chested Tristan
Drinks their death
As a New Year's Eve poem

Let's wake up to the miracle in us
Beyond the shape of expectation
Timeless, palindromic, undulating
To the unda our whimper trembles
Upon the reflection of a fixed star
Lost in its own nocturnal pilgrimage

Let our palms unite the serpentine loveliness
In a cleansing lust
As nuggets of light bathing in East China sea
And set, rocking forth
And rolling back

Upon un-parted, departed, and patroness waters

And when in our gourde the sanguinal wine dries,
Let's dismount, love, the beast
In others we found
For love, the lonely rider
In the ideal agony of the wound
Healed only by the very blow
To which it is born
Will swallow its wooden whip
And, on the balcony of a low-income housing complex,
Break its own back

—*September 15, 1997*
Korean Air #84
New York to Seoul

Alil

Large shoulders covered a body in need for shelter
Hands, of the daily chores dry and thick
Held her face as young men hold aging hips
On summer nights while fruit bats arabesque over them

He brought her chest to his back pink on black
To calm the river within that shores often exist
To hold the flow not the waves lonesome moments make
When hope is under six feet of dark dirts and still drawing rainbows
Over frightened faces large callous hands hold
As a sound sparrow chick make
When they fall of the nest and break an unformed wing
And learn about the wind from branches fallen rather than the wind itself
As her face rests upon the palm and in his commonly brown eyes she founds the unspoken hold Large shoulders can have when the body needs shelter
When the body is yours as a child in a world
Where children dream of large shoulders to cover them in peace and in calm
And where brown eyes look through them in adoration

—*June 16, 1998*

The Intern Was Lost

.... I picked her up and cleaned the gravel imbedded in her
Jaw
For of the fall her eyes were dark and her scent that I had Known so
well
Was gone
It was a half moon when on the pavement of a cold city
A woman with silver hair and a shaky hand found her
A woman with no name
A woman with no face
For where she once had dark brows part of her inside was
Now out
With gravel stuck to it
That I tried to clean
As we often do when the return home is no more possible
When the accidental thought of happiness
Wraps around the entrails of a present disfiguring itself in Harmony
And in vain
While we force the hand to open
The fingers to relax
To release a ring
The last circle of a personal mandala made of the dark
Grains of a lifetime
Upon which the putrid breath of destiny would exhale one Night
When the moon is half of what it can be
When the people of hatred and pain
Are full
As she lies upon her once known face
Upon the cold gravel
Next to an oil stained asphalt curve
Of a city
Where Singing birds are served as desert
To all Thanksgiving dinners
No one will wash your face tonight
Except the light from a moon
That will be there again next day
While you will not

—August 5, 1998

Praying in an Old Temple

It is the dance
Of last chance
Which we will regret
Tomorrow

Hold me and smile
As girls with breasts do
During a slow dance
Under the morning dew

Run your fingers
On my face and please linger
As when I placed white rose petals
On your freckled breasts

My heart is cold, mellimou,
Of the wait for you
See, great rivers have met their time
When the space of the moment got by

Return.
There is still time to dance
The valse of last chance

And then regret
That we had made
Our past
Last

—October 1, 1998

Chateau Moussas, 1996

For the word to touch its own shound and rhyme
Lips, hips, and strong coffee should provide
The smell of love and tobacco over the wooden bed
And a window should open, by the winds, often

To wake up without having dozed off
Among people you once know
Like the fear you now know
After knowing them

For the call to become a song
Bare feet on the balcony must touch
Bare feet resting upon the railing
Catching morning rays with toes painted
In pastel, as the moment is
In red, as the moment was
In harmony as dark coffee swirls with rich cream
On the balcony where bare feet walk know back to the room

To wake up without having dozed away
Among people you thought you knew
Like the fear you will always have
After knowing them

—October 18, 1998
Miami to Buenos Aires
8:14 a.m.

112

Old Vine, New Wine

It was in the garden of small secrets
In late August one morning
When you breast touched a though I had of you
The day before
Next to a Lilac bush shaped like a name
You gave to the mist upon the pond in Aniline Park

Like a weed growing in a wall crack
Like a cricket in a damp and dark basement
I shared my space with the whirling sounds
Your bare feet made upon my space

It was in the garden of no secrets
That upon your hands an aging dove resposed
Its aching plumage as if snow flakes
Slow and cold snow flakes
Lost in August on a misty day

When your white and ocld toes touched my time
I was in thought
I was in pain
I was alone
Like a week in the crack of an old wall
That divides itslef into a reflective silence
Where sounds bounce upon themselves and fill the mis in rain

Do you remember, say
When your freckled breast touched the hope I had of you
For the next day
Next to the freshly painted wall, in white
Where you picked my sould in your uncarressed palms
And while arching of the mist trembling lips

You said
"I love you, I love you not"

The garden of small secrets, love
Is now all weeds

—October 17, 1998
American Airlines, Flight #637
Washington to Miami
6:16 p.m.

Wormwood in Spice

The paint was still wet when upon a midnight blue sky
Crows flew in silence golden husks in their beaks
As if the poet in Amsterdam, who burned his amber pipe in
Vain
To rope in blue clouds thoughts of harvest, in the midday sun.

My mind is in travel, my flight is in wonder.
"Did my name spell in bright red? Or was it purple brown?"
I touch my lips in a motion that seems that of a brush
Upon paint still we, as the yellow becomes a sound then a
Macabre dance.

The sea! It breaks upon the wall of mossy rocks and runs the
Distance
Where surviving waves become shiny crows, become the
Reddish beard
Of the poet still burning his tongue as he burns his briar pipe. In
vain!
For the muses will only make love to each other, by rubbing
Their aging breasts

In honey, in neroli, in almond and in absinth
And they will let down their hair, red, brown, green, purple,
And old
To cover the marks sailors' sparse teeth have left upon their
Arching shoulders.
The Muses are tired tonight; the muses have been tired for
Awhile now.

The paint was still wet when I brushed an image of pain
Upon a yellow house on a dirt street, where upon a wooden
Chair I found
The poet, swallowing his own ulcerated tongue in hunger

While harlots delivered the unwanted child of his dreams upon
Soiled sheets
And bathe him, in the sweet water the just broke,
As crows flew in silence, golden harvest's husks in their beaks....

—December 1, 1998
The National Gallery of Arts
Washington, D.C.
The Van Gogh Exhibit